INTO THE DEPTHS

TALES FROM THE LIGHTHOUSE
BOOK 3

D.L. STRAND

Storyteller's
PUBLISHING

For My Girls - Monika, Alyssa, & Kayla

1

THE END

Jessie lay dying in my lap.

We sped through the dark. Tearing through twisting, hopeless streets that were once familiar, but now seemed to lead everywhere except where we needed to go. Max forced her truck through the tiny roads that wound through Santa Carla, throwing us one way and back, squealing around turns and bucking over curbs. Gram sat next to her, slumped over in the passenger seat as I rode in the back with my legs braced against the walls, struggling to be a still, safe space in the bed of the careening vehicle, while Jessie's blood seeped through the towel wrapped around her head and onto my lap, then puddled on the corrugated steel floor beneath me.

I begged to God or the Universe, or whatever passed for a higher power in this fucked up world to save them both somehow. Change this nightmare to a dream or a fevered hallucination from which I'd awaken, trembling, drenched in sweat, but relieved to find that in the end, everything was okay, the sun had come up after all, Jessie and Gram were alive, and Lester was just a figment of my overactive imagination.

The truck screamed around a corner, and swerving out of the turn, struck a curb or speed bump or something, and launched into the air. We were weightless for a moment and Jessie's head lifted from my lap, then dropped back down without so much as a flutter from her eyelashes. I couldn't tell if she breathed or not.

Finally, Max sped onto the main road, drifting freely from lane to lane. We pulled hard to the right, jolted into the parking lot, and jerked to a stop in front of the hospital's emergency entrance.

Jessie lay still. So still.

As much as I prayed for this to not be real—as hard as I tried to deny the reality lying on my lap—deep down I knew this world wasn't that kind.

Max jumped out of the car and ran inside.

A moment later, she rushed back with hospital workers hurrying behind her, pushing gurneys in front of them.

I tried to lift Jessie, but her body hung limp and heavy.

"Keep still," one of them commanded as he vaulted into the truck and knelt beside me. Pulling a penlight from his shirt pocket, he shined it into her eyes, then placed a stethoscope on her chest and listened for a long moment. Time stopped. He withdrew the device, then gently scooped her up and handed her down to his co-worker who laid her on the stretcher. "What happened?" He asked.

I watched as Jessie and Gram were wheeled away. Without her weight on me, I felt cold. Shivers rocked my body. Through trembling lips, with a voice weak and distant in my own ears, I replied. "It was my fault. It was all my fault."

2

HOW IT STARTED - THE PHONE CALL

"So, you don't like movies?" I said, sitting on the floor of the hallway, cradling the phone between my cheek and shoulder. I'd finally healed enough from Lester's last attack so I could go out on my own. The doctor said it'd been a minor miracle that the bullet had only nicked my spleen. At the time, I hadn't felt so lucky. It'd hurt - a lot. But now that I could go out again, it felt damned great to be alive, especially since I had a girlfriend. Imagine. A girlfriend. Me!

It'd been a few weeks since Lester'd trapped us in that house up in the hills above Santa Carla: Gram, Jessie, Max, Bunny (Max's stepmother) and I were lucky to have escaped alive. Things hadn't gone so well for Max's dad. Being a police detective had made him the perfect host for Lester's twisted, psychopathic spirit. In the end, Max had saved us all, but she'd had to kill her father to do it.

Jessie had visited or called every day since, but we'd only been on one date so far, and that was before all that stuff happened.

She laughed. "I can hear your gears turning, Sam.

You've been cooped up for three weeks. Aren't you tired of just sitting around? Let's get out. Walk around. See people."

What was she talking about? Movies were the perfect choice for a date; they provided a set length of time during which we'd be stuck together - and I didn't have to be clever. Without that distraction, she might realize what a loser I was. Oh, and the kicker - a great movie would reflect well on me.

"Look, if you'd prefer to see a movie—" she began.

"No. We can do something else," I said - caving. What choice did I have?

"Okay, but I have a caveat."

"A what?"

"A caveat; *The Empire Strikes Back* comes out in May. I know it sounds nerdy, but I want to see it with you."

"That might be... cool, I guess," I said casually, but inside, I exploded like the Death Star, or Alderaan, or the TIE fighter when Luke shot it with the Millennium Falcon's laser cannon, or - you get the idea. She didn't just want to see the movie, she wanted to see it with me, and it wasn't coming out for another four months, which meant she thought we'd still be together. Two very bitchin' things.

"How about Pleasure Pizza?" she suggested.

"Across from the bookstore on Pacific?"

"Bookshop Santa Carla - we can go there after." I glanced at my shelves, stuffed with titles by Alan Dean Foster, Anne McCaffrey, Raymond Feist, and others.

"Pizza and books. Great."

"Perfect. See you then."

Up to now, any girl willing to talk to me rated high on my list - but as I hung up the phone, I realized Jessie might be this geek's dream girl.

3

PLANS CHANGE

I WAS IN THE BATHROOM, COMBING MY HAIR, WHEN THE front door slammed. Wrapped in a towel, I stepped out to say hi. Gram had been so busy, off doing whatever, we hadn't seen each other in a few days.

She walked past me with her shoulders hunched, her face drawn and her gaze lowered. She looked beaten, shorter, frail. Her purple velour track suit should've brightened up her appearance, but it made her seem pale and washed out.

"Hey, Gram."

She patted my arm without saying a word. Didn't even look at me.

Troubled, I stepped back into the bathroom.

We'd looked out for each other since my grandpa died a couple years before. His death hit both of us hard. The shock and sadness had taken her ability to speak. For a while, all we had was each other.

After the nightmare up in Boulder Creek, it seemed we'd put the worst of our troubles behind us. She'd become more independent, going out on her own for hours each day. Best of all, she'd started talking again.

I picked up my comb then lowered it without touching a hair on my head, and peaked around the door, into her room. Gram lay on top of her bed with her eyes closed. She appeared to be sleeping already.

Just then, the phone rang.

"Hey, is everything okay?" It was Jessie. She continued before I could respond. "I sound like the crazy girlfriend, I know, but I had this weird feeling that something was wrong."

Could've knocked me over with a feather, was one of Gram's favorite sayings, and it described precisely how I felt. "That's bizarre."

"I know. I'm sorry I called. I'll see you at the pizza place."

"No, it's… Hold on." I pulled the phone into my room and closed the door. "Are you still there?" I asked.

"Yeah."

I kept my voice low. "Gram just got home. Something's off."

"Do you want a raincheck?"

"No. I totally want to see you, it's just…" I was torn. Maybe Gram was fine, but maybe she wasn't.

"How about if I come over, then we can hang out, and keep an eye on her?" Jessie said.

"That'd be great. Are you sure?"

"Absolutely, as long as I'm not intruding. How's six? I'll bring dinner."

"Awesome." I was really liking this whole, having-a-girlfriend thing.

4

THE DATE

With Jessie coming over, I not only had to make myself presentable, I also needed to straighten up my room, the bathroom, the kitchen - most of the house, really. With Gram away so much, the place was more relaxed than usual.

After straightening things up, I took a glass of water into Gram's room. She lay on top of her covers, sleeping hard. I covered her with a blanket and closed the door, then sat down at the kitchen table to wait, not sure what to do with myself.

Jessie and I had grown close over the weeks, but I felt nervous. It was only our second date, after all.

Her car pulled up a few minutes early and rather than wait for her to knock, I rushed out to meet her.

She was reaching into the passenger seat of her jeep as I approached, then straightened and pivoted with a pizza box and a six-pack of Coke in her arms. She looked surprised - the good kind of surprised.

I held my hands out to take her burden. Instead, she set our dinner on the hood and greeted me with a hug and a lingering kiss, then leaned back. Our arms were still locked around each other.

"Nice to see you, too. How's Gram?" She asked.

"Sleeping." I let go of her and grabbed the food.

"That's good, right?"

"I guess." I shrugged. "How did you know?"

"About Gram?" She snagged the cans off the top of the box, and with her free arm wrapped around my waist, we started back toward the house. "Like I said, just a feeling."

"So, you're psychic?" After the things we'd experienced, anything was possible.

She shrugged. "Maybe."

My spider-sense tingled, but I brushed it off, and hurried ahead to open the door. I waved her in with a flourish.

"Such a gentleman," she teased.

"Chivalry isn't dead."

"Nope. It just smells funny," she said as she stepped inside.

"Monty Python?" I asked.

"Frank Zappa."

Zappa. My girlfriend quoted Zappa.

Keeping our voices down, we made for the kitchen.

I took out the plates and opened the silverware drawer.

She cocked her head, as if I was doing something silly.

"Fork, bad?"

"It's pizza," she said.

"Good point." We filled our plates and headed out to the living room where we wouldn't have to be so quiet and settled in on the couch.

"Did she say anything? What was she doing today?" Jessie asked.

I shrugged. "No idea."

"She's a strong lady. She's probably fine."

I nodded, still worried this was more than simple fatigue.

"How's your pizza?" She asked.

I'm pretty sure that when Moses came down from the mountain carrying his tablets, he held them out flat, and on top of each one was a large, deep-dish, Chicago-style sausage and mushroom pie, hand-tossed by God. Oh, and the eleventh commandment said: Thou Shalt not defile thy pizza with dead fish. Look it up. I'm sure I'm right.

Tonight, for the first time, I found my appetite unmoved.

"You're not hungry?" She'd already finished one slice and was working on her second.

I brought a piece to my mouth, but couldn't bring myself to take a bite. Instead, I set it back down. I couldn't help it. I was worried.

"Are we having pizza?" a familiar voice asked.

I turned around, and saw Gram, her hair jutted haphazardly from one side of her head, and lay flat against the other. She looked better, though. Rested. She smiled.

"Would you like to join us?" Jessie asked.

"Let me go freshen up a little."

Jessie got up and, as she walked past me, scooped my plate off the table and put it back into my hands. "Don't let it get cold."

Gram joined us in the living room. But where Jessie and I had Cokes, she'd grabbed a bottle of beer.

"Jessie, honey, you didn't need to bring dinner."

"I kinda did. Ask Sam."

I didn't look up. I didn't want her to know how concerned I was.

"I ruined your plans, didn't I?" said Gram.

"No," Jessie and I said in unison.

"Sam was worried," Jessie admitted, "but this ended up being a pleasant night, didn't it?"

"Yes, it did, dear. Thank you."

Before long, pizza bones littered the box, and we were stuffed.

"Well, thank you both." Gram stood and gathered the plates. "I'm going to clean this up, and you're going to go have some fun."

"No, I've got this—" Jessie began.

She stopped mid-sentence when she saw the steely look on Gram's face. "You're sure?"

"Quite sure. Now run off. I don't want to miss Wheel of Fortune."

"Since when do you watch…?"

She trained the same icy gaze on me.

"You're sure you're okay?"

Again, with the look.

"All right. Let's go," I said.

"I grabbed my wallet and key, kissed Gram on the cheek, and followed Jessie outside. "Maybe we can catch a movie."

"Funny." Jessie said, as I closed the door behind us.

5

A GIFT FOR GRAM

Santa Carla is a tourist town, but with an edge - a bohemian flair, I suppose. We've got shopping, restaurants, and bars, then there's the beach, the surf, the boardwalk, biker gangs, drugs, hookers - something for everyone.

"So, where to?" I asked. She'd parked her car on Front Street. Evening shoppers trickled by.

"Let's walk for a while." I said.

She took my hand, and we strolled in silence for a couple of blocks, not really caring which direction we took, enjoying each other's company - window shopping, or window gazing, as we didn't really want anything we saw. That's what I thought, anyway.

Jessie paused in front of a new place: The smell of wax and something else, maybe sulfur, assaulted my nose. The sign read, *Flaming Peace - a candle-making workshop*.

"Ooh, let's go in." She opened the door and pulled me after her.

The smell intensified once we entered, and I was hit with a variety of aromas. It was like a symphony, but all the instruments were out of tune. It was stifling, claustrophobic.

The place was a hodgepodge of old, discarded furniture, thrift store tables, and reclaimed shelving units loaded with glass jars - mostly empty.

An older man with a threadbare beard stood in the middle of the room, all long limbs, bony elbows, and a paunchy gut. His smile was almost as fake as his blond ponytail. He wore a tie-dyed t-shirt, with a large purple pendant hanging from a thin leather strap around his neck. In most other towns, he'd have stuck out like a nonconforming, liberal, commie-pinko thumb; an orphaned flower child; a sad hippy dropout who'd been left behind to make way for the *I-me-mine* generation of yuppies that came after. Here in Santa Carla though, he was just another struggling entrepreneur.

Jessie led me to him. "We'd like to make a candle."

"We would?" This was news to me.

She squeezed my hand.

"Cool." He rubbed his hands together hungrily. "Have you been here before?"

"First time," she said with a note of excitement, as though this was something we'd been dying to do.

"I'll get you set up."

He grabbed a smallish, off-white fabric bag and led us to a table laid out with empty jars of different sizes and several lengths of string - which I assumed were wicks. He turned the bag over and out thumped several chunks of wax - all black. "Have fun," he said, then headed to the back of the store.

Several other couples stood at similar tables. A middle-aged man met my gaze, looking as confused as I felt.

"So, what do we do?" Why were we here? What happened to the bookstore?

"It's fun. Gram will love it."

"Gram?"

"We should do something nice for her. Don't you think she'll like it?" Jessie sounded worried. My face must've betrayed me.

A black candle in a jar? "I'm sure she'll love it," I said, as convincingly as I could.

"You think she'll hate it." She caught me.

"I didn't say that." But I was thinking it.

"You hate it."

"No." What was happening?

She looked at me suspiciously. "You think it's stupid."

"No, it'll be fun. Show me. What do we do?" I reached for one of the jars with the sinking feeling that the night was slipping away from me.

"You think I'm stupid."

"No, I don't." Crazy, maybe.

Her volume increased. "You're so fucking selfish. I don't know why I thought you'd like this."

"No," I said, "Seriously. I think it's great," I lied. "C'mon, let's make a candle."

"You don't think this is great. All you want—"

"Is to have a nice evening." I interjected. "C'mon, let's make a Goddamned candle." I grabbed a wax chunk and tried to jam it into the jar. It wouldn't fit.

"You don't have to yell at me. God! I'm just trying to do something nice…"

The other customers stared at us. Everything I said added gas to her fire. Desperate, I picked up another piece. That didn't fit, either. "What's the fucking point of this?" Did I say that out-loud?

She continued, "She's your grandmother. I just thought you'd want to do something thoughtful, but if you can't be bothered—"

I slammed the wax down onto the table. "Where the fuck do you get off—?"

There was a light tap on my shoulder. I turned to see a woman - slight, shorter than Jessie, her gray hair pulled back in a loose bun. "Maybe I can help." She shoved something into my face. It prickled my upper lip.

I recoiled and tried to bat it away.

"Which do you like better? She jabbed something else at me. I had a glimpse of green and purple, then it disappeared under my nose.

I tried to back away, but she kept it there. She did the same with Jessie.

"Isn't that a lovely fragrance?"

"I-I don't care…" A scent of lavender caught my attention and I forgot what I was going to say.

"Rosemary?" Jessie asked. "I-love that smell."

"So, what're you making?" the lady asked.

I looked down at the table. The objects held no attraction or repulsion for me. They had no meaning at all.

Jessie and I regarded each other, puzzled.

The lady handed us the herbs, then leaned in and whispered into my ear. "It's a beautiful night. You should go for a walk," and with that, she moved away.

An idea popped into my head. "How about ice cream?"

Jessie's brow wrinkled.

I pressed my case. "We could go to Marianne's."

She started to shake her head.

I jumped in before she could reply. "You're right. Marianne's is too far to walk. Let's go to the place on Cedar."

"Penny's?"

"Sure, Penny's. Whatever you want."

"Then we can come back?" She asked.

God, no. "Of course," I lied. "If that's what you want."

She let me guide her toward the door. As we stepped out into the cool night air, I looked back over my shoulder and watched the strange woman intercept the shop's owner. I let the door close silently behind us.

6

THE WITCH

With my hand on her back, I guided Jessie down Front Street, then turned right onto Church, steeling glances her way. She still looked confused.

Just a block later, we made a right onto Cedar.

From the corner, I could see Penny's—a throwback to the early nineteen hundreds - a small, free-standing building with stark white stucco walls and a Spanish tile roof. Tables perched on the tiny step-up porch, behind thin peppermint stick columns. Inside, light flooded through the windows framed in dark wood. A clerk wiped the counter as a couple stared at the menu overhead.

Jessie paused, holding the rosemary under her nose. "What the hell just happened?"

"I think we had our first fight." I said.

"It seemed like a brilliant idea."

"The fight?"

She swatted my shoulder. "The candle, but now..."

She was acting more like herself, but I didn't want to point that out, or mention how bug-shit crazy she'd been just a few moments earlier.

"C'mon.".

She hesitated. "I don't think I want any ice cream, though."

I stepped back onto the sidewalk. "Are you sure?"

"I think I'd rather just walk."

The idea of two huge scoops - vanilla and bing cherry - jammed into a large waffle cone, evaporated. I gazed back at the shop. The couple stepped out onto the porch, ice creams in hand. A sweet aroma followed them out into the air.

"You're disappointed."

I sighed dramatically. "No. I'm fine."

"We can still get you one."

"Don't worry about me. I—I'll be okay."

"Seriously, we can get you an ice cream."

"No, really. I didn't - I didn't really want one." My voice was barely a whisper. It might've cracked.

"I swear to God!" She dragged me across the quiet street, onto the sidewalk, and didn't stop pulling until we stood in front of the counter. "Tell the nice lady what you want."

Laughing, I gave her my order.

"Anything for you?" she asked Jessie.

"A new boyfriend!"

"Nothing for her." I pulled out my wallet.

She put her hand on mine. "There's no way you're paying."

"I'm pretty sure I'll be paying for it later," I joked. I glanced down at my wallet. There was a business card sticking out of it. I pulled it out. It read,

The Serpent's Eye
Fortunes & Metaphysical Supplies
Madame Sylvia - Proprietor

"What's that?"

I didn't remember seeing it before. I shrugged and stuffed it into my pocket. "No idea."

The clerk presented my cone wrapped in wax paper and accepted Jessie's cash.

"Keep the change." Jessie said as she stuffed her wallet back into her purse. "Happy?"

I was already in the middle of my third lick. "Mmm-hmm."

As I pulled napkins from the chrome dispenser, she grabbed my hand and stole a taste for herself.

"Oh, that is good." She continued to go after it.

"You want me to get you one?" I asked.

"Mmm-mmm." She mumbled negatively as she continued devouring my treat.

I brushed the top scoop against her nose.

"Hey!"

I held out a napkin. "Truce?"

"For now." She giggled, wiping off her nose.

We left and wandered, not thinking about direction. After a while, people became scarce. As we traveled east, away from the seaside, charming shops gave way to more office-like buildings. Each one was just like the last.

We strolled quietly, simply enjoying the night.

With the ice cream devoured, we dropped our napkins into a wire-frame trash bin, and stood in front of a shop that didn't fit the conservative neighborhood. The garish awning read *The Serpent's Eye - Fortunes & Metaphysical Supplies.*

I pulled the card out of my pocket. "No way," I said, and showed it to Jessie.

I'd always been a sucker for sleight of hand, card tricks, that sort of thing. I tilted my head toward the place. "You wanna?"

"Seriously?"

"What could go wrong?"

She slapped my shoulder and pushed open the red-painted door. A bell above it announced our entrance as we stepped inside.

A large red carpet covered all but the edge of the floor. An assortment of wood and glass display cases lined every wall. Books, statuettes, candles, incense; all kinds of strange things decorated the tables, but nowhere did I find the trick card decks and dribble cups you usually find in a magician's shop. It dawned on me that this might be a completely different kind of magic.

A table at the back of the room caught my attention, as it was loaded with crystal balls of various sizes. As I approached, my reflection in the largest one distorted, stretched, and then flipped upside down. I leaned closer, and a soft light winked behind me in the glass. I scanned the room, but except for a couple of lit candles, there was nothing to explain it. I turned back to the globe. The light pulsed again, brighter now, with a steady rhythm, and as I stared, it seemed to intensify. I realized that rather than pulse, the beam seemed to rotate, like a…

"Feeling better?"

I jumped.

A woman stood next to me. Where had she come from? I'd been so engrossed in the glass ball.

"I-I was just…" There was something pulling at me, but like a half-formed thought I lost the thread. I returned my gaze to the crystal. The image was gone.

"You'll have to forgive my boyfriend. Him no talk good." Jessie stepped forward. "I think we met earlier. I'm Jessie"

I realized it was the woman from the candle shop.

The lady smiled and held out her hand. "I'm glad you stopped by. I'm Sylvia."

I held out my hand, "Sam Freman."

"Freman - the name's familiar. Do we know each other?"

"I don't think so."

Jessie brought the little twig of rosemary out of her pocket.

"Curious?"

I took the lavender out of my own.

"You are feeling better, aren't you?"

"Better?" Jessie asked.

"She's definitely feeling better," I said.

"I don't understand," said Jessie.

"In the candle shop…?" I prompted.

"Are you talking about our fight?"

"Sylvia shoved it under your nose, remember?"

"Rosemary and lavender are wonderful for calming the nerves," Sylvia said. "You two seemed to need it."

"I'm not following," I said.

"Sometimes, a simple change of focus can help when people are affected by - certain things."

"Things?"

"Let's just say Marvin was messing around where he shouldn't have been."

Jessie asked, "Who's Marvin? What things?"

"The owner of the candle shop. He won't do it again."

Jessie drew the rosemary through her fingers, then held it to her nose again.

"Soothing, isn't it? People get so wrapped up in their little dramas. They don't know how much nature can heal, just by inhaling a fragrance, or…" From her own pocket, she drew out a large purple gem suspended from a leather strap. It looked similar - very similar - to the one the candle shop owner had been wearing. She lowered it so it hovered just above the tabletop. "See how, just by shining a light, we can open a window?"

Sure enough, the room's dim light refracted through the gem onto the wood, surrounding the pendant with rectangles that looked like little purple windows.

"What might we see if we could look inside?" She raised it again, so the light twinkled in my eyes. "Maybe different realms that inhabit the same space we do, separated by light and shadow." She put the pendant away.

I couldn't say why, but I felt relaxed. Peaceful.

Jessie and I regarded each other and smiled.

"That's amazing."

The woman laughed. "Well, it's not magic. Just simple biology, aromatherapy, focused awareness. Maybe a touch of hypnosis. Marvin's an idiot. He should've taken a class in marketing."

I recalled the overwhelming smell of the shop. How I'd felt tense, closed in. "So, he cast a spell on us?"

"As if." Sylvia laughed. "It was just a simple charm."

"Wait, magic is real?" I thought all I needed to worry about were ghosts.

"Would you like to see for yourself?"

"You're not going to turn him into a newt, are you?" Jessie joked.

Sylvia shrugged. "I can tell your fortune, if you like."

"We don't have any money," Jessie said.

Sylvia rolled her eyes. "Of course you have money. You're on a date. It doesn't matter, though. No charge."

"Seriously?" I said.

"I'm not getting any more business tonight, anyway."

"How do you know?"

Sylvia's eyes flashed as she whispered whispered, "Psychic," she said, then added, "Oh, and I closed the shop ten minutes ago." She pointed to the sign in the window.

How had I missed that?

"Besides, I feel I owe it to you after Marvin almost ruined your night."

Jessie was intrigued. "You wanna?"

I wasn't sure. "It's getting late."

Jessie gave me a little shove. "C'mon. It'll be fun. It's just a simple reading, right?"

Sylvia nodded.

And my nightmare with Lester had started out as a simple boat ride. Still...

"What could go wrong?" she smiled.

That was the thing. I didn't know what could happen. Ouija boards were supposed to open you up to spirits and demons and stuff. At least, that's what the Moral Majority was saying on TV. What if this was like that? On the other hand, what if I was being silly? Was I 'pussing out' like Max would say? "How does it work?" I asked.

Sylvia crossed to a curtain , and slid it sideways, revealing a closet-sized room with a small table and chairs. A piece of black fabric was draped over the table, deco-rated with a large five-pointed star, set inside a double circle. There were runes scribed along the edge. It reminded me of the graffiti I'd seen covering the walls in the lighthouse. My stomach tightened.

"Usually, I give the customer the choice of what tool they'd like me to use: tarot, runes, et cetera, but tonight I feel drawn to the crystal ball. Is that okay?"

"Sure. Fine," I said. What difference did it make?

She hefted the large clear globe and placed it before her, then struck a match to light a well-burnt, white candle, and a small incense cone, from which a luxurious smoke poured out, cascading down the ceramic skull upon which it sat - a sort of smokefall, that filled the eye holes and mouth before it writhed out and slithered onto the table. The aroma, at once earthy and ethereal, caressed my senses.

She took a deep breath, closed her eyes, and laid her hands on the table, with her palms facing up. "Each of you, take my hand."

We did. "Close your eyes and try to clear your mind. Breathe in the incense. Drift in the scent. Allow your thoughts to simply float." She inhaled deeply again. "You're in a safe space. Relax. Let your…"

As she spoke, Jessie and I shared a glance and a smile. I felt foolish—and for some maybe a little exposed.

"There's something… Oh, no. Wait, I think–yes, I see. No. Okay, that's better." Her words stumbled out in fits and starts and I wondered if I was ever going to be involved in the telling of my fortune.

"There's someone—a man." She looked up from the globe. Her tone was serious. Her look, grave. "This isn't what I was expecting."

"Is it bad?" Jessie took my hand in hers.

Sylvia returned her eyes to the crystal. "He's angry. No, it's more. I sense rage. Uncontrollable. Intense. We don't have to continue."

"Cool." I was all for stopping.

Jessie thought otherwise. "If there's something coming, we should know about it."

Sylvia continued. "I've never seen anything like this. I sense - I don't know, there's a—it's hard to explain—a hopping sensation. First, he's one place, then another."

The casket-sized room shrank. I felt hot. Sweat trickled down the side of my face. My stomach clenched.

"He jumps from one place to—no, not a place—this doesn't make any sense." She squinted, leaning in closer.

"It's like he's dying over and over again, feeding off pain and… death, and then he moves on to another…"

Jessie gripped my hand tight. "Is this current, or in the past?"

Sylvia continued. "There's someone close to you. Her name is Dorothy. She's your…grandmother? She's warning you, 'Stay away.'"

"But Gram's alive," Jessie blurted.

"I see her fighting. Overpowered. Slipping away. He's using her to—"

"Okay!" I said. "Reading's over." I bolted to my feet, almost upsetting the table in the cramped space. I practically lifted Jessie out of her chair so I could escape the tiny room.

"Sam—!"

I took her hand and made for the door.

She hesitated.

"Come on. We're done." I said.

I didn't wait for her to reply. I just wanted—no, needed to get out of there. I threw open the door and escaped out into the night, with Jessie trailing behind.

7

THE TALK

Despite the hour, lights blazed in the house. Jessie's jeep drove off as I closed the door behind.

Gram waited for me in the den. "I like her."

"Jessie? Me too." I tried to sound cheerful. I headed into the kitchen.

I kept talking as I opened the fridge and grabbed a carton of milk, "So, what're you doing up? After your day, I thought you'd turn in early." I closed the fridge and jumped back, startled. She'd been standing right behind it.

I pushed on. "Do you want some?"

"I'm fine, dear." She held up a short glass of whisky. I didn't know we had whisky.

"Hitting the hard stuff?" What was with the drinking?

I crossed to the cupboard, and took out a large glass.

She waited while I poured and returned the milk to the fridge.

"We should talk," she said, her voice heavy.

"Okay, shoot." I was still feeling weird after my date.

"Would you like a snack? I can make grilled cheese."

"Sure," I said enthusiastically.

"I'll get out the pan. Why don't you slice some cheese?"

It'd been a long time since we'd cooked together.

We chatted while we worked. I told her about my night, omitting the witchy stuff. I wasn't sure how I felt about that yet, but was leaning toward being seriously freaked out. We also discussed my plans for the upcoming semester, classes, driving lessons—things like that.

She sliced a hunk of butter and slapped it into the pan. It sizzled vigorously. "Oops." She lowered the fire and tilted the pan one way and then the other, making the butter slide around as it melted, filling the room with its enticing odor. She added two more pats, then dropped the sandwiches on top.

There's nothing complicated about making grilled cheese, but watching the casually skillful way she worked was comforting. This kitchen was the heart of our home, and she provided its rhythm, its life, doing everything simply, with love.

We gabbed the whole time, words and laughter coming easily.

I hadn't been hungry before, but now, my stomach rumbled.

Finally, the sandwiches were ready, and with quick flicks of her spatula, they landed on our plates.

I poured another milk for myself, and we sat down to enjoy.

After talking almost nonstop, the room went silent, and the only sounds were our teeth breaking the crispy, buttery surface of the toasted bread.

Gram would tell you it was the extra butter that made the difference, but she got everything right: sourdough bread, two different cheeses - never that pre-wrapped, artificial stuff either - a touch of mustard, then toasted just right - light on the edges, darkened to a deep golden brown in the center, with cheese oozing out the sides.

"So good," I said, picking the last few crumbs off my plate.

She held her own plate out for me; on it sat the remaining half of her sandwich.

I shook my head, but we both knew it was an act and so I accepted it gratefully.

Afterward, we sat at the table, soaking in the afterglow of the snack. "Oh, what did you want to talk about?" I asked.

She hesitated, then smiled. "I thought we just did."

I took the plates over to the sink. "I guess we did," I said, laughing.

She grabbed the frying pan off the stove, elbowing me out of the way. "I've got this."

I kissed her on the cheek. "You're so pushy. Thank you."

"Sleep tight," she replied, not looking up.

8

LESSONS

"WE'LL START YOU IN PRE-ALGEBRA..." THE SCHOOL councilor sat across from me, her bifocals reflecting the green light of the monitor. "Your English skills are solid, so we'll put you in Advanced Comp. Combine that with California History, and oh, you haven't picked a Phys. Ed. class yet." She slid the course catalog in front of me.

I thought I was done with P.E. This was college—okay, junior college, but still—weight lifting, locker rooms, group showers... Some of my worst, most humiliating experiences had happened in P.E. Bullying was a team sport, after all. Couldn't I postpone it—maybe take something fun and useful instead, like Rhythmic Video Gaming?

I skimmed the list; Aerobics, Badminton, Baseball, Basketball, Strength Training, Total Fitness, it all sounded awful. I turned the page; Water Polo, Weight Training... I flipped it back - this time, something caught my eye and I read it out loud; "Tae-kwon-do - This course utilizes martial arts techniques including kicks, punches, blocks, and defensive techniques in a cardio exercise program to enhance cardiorespiratory fitness and personal safety."

In other words, a class to help ward off swirlies and nuclear wedgies. I pointed to it.

She punched a few buttons. "Done."

She hit another button, and the printer chewed up some green-and-white striped computer paper, and spit out my schedule. She ripped it out and tore off the perforated edges. "Take this to the cashier."

"That's it?"

"Do you need a parking permit?"

I shook my head.

She smiled. "Then we'll see you in February."

In high school, my goals had been to watch as much TV as I could, avoid homework, and try to get home from school without someone kicking my ass or stuffing me into a trash can.

I'd thought of the junior college as a small step up from high school. The name implied it came with training wheels or something. But the woman had spoken to me as if I was an adult, with no judgment about my transcript, no urging to 'apply myself.'

It felt good to take a step toward my future on my own, even if I didn't have a clue where that future might lead.

I exited the building and leaned against one of the heavy concrete planters, waiting for Max. It was January and we were between semesters, so traffic was light.

The high school campus had always reminded me of a prison, with the buildings forming an enclosed rectangle in the middle, a recreation area outside of that, and everything enclosed by a tall, wire fence.

This school on the other hand, was built high above Santa Carla and provided sweeping views of the town, The Boardwalk, and the ocean beyond.

I zipped my coat to ward off the cold wind blowing off the water.

A hulking student approached. His neon green tank top glowed against his tanned skin and strained to contain the bulk of his massive chest and back. His hair, blacker than nature intended, was swept back, high off his forehead, and hung to his shoulders in back.

I knew him. Derrick Ryan was one of Mitch Kavenaugh's lackeys who'd made my life miserable in high school. I was caught in the open, with no group to lose myself in, no hallway to duck down. I braced myself for the, "Hey, ya little faggot. Kill anyone's parents today?" jibe. They loved to poke fun at the fact my folks were dead. Go figure.

Instead, he simply nodded and walked by as if I was a normal person, someone he recognized, someone worth acknowledging. Maybe things would be different here. I relaxed as I watched him swagger to his red Camaro and speed out of the parking lot.

A few moments later, a weathered two-door convertible rumbled around the horseshoe-shaped driveway. Dents marred the front fenders. Rust crept down the once-white paint from the corner of the windshield, and one headlight was cracked, so it looked like it'd been punched in the eye. "Hey, Dipshit, you gonna sit there all day?" It was Max. I smiled as I approached.

"Kinda great, right?" she said, gesturing to the car.

"No." I laughed. "What is it?" I asked.

"It's a car," she snarked.

I rolled my eyes. "What's the make?"

She scoffed. "This is a nineteen sixty-one Pontiac Tempest, and it's badass." She wore a *Surfin' Santa Carla* baseball cap and grease-stained coveralls with the name *Larry* embroidered on the pocket. The afternoon sun shone off the piercings in her ears, eyebrow, nose, and lip, despite the dark smudges on her face. She scooted over the passenger side, and gestured toward the steering wheel.

"You want me to drive this?" Suddenly, I felt very nervous.

She scoffed. "You didn't think I was gonna let you drive my truck, did you?"

"Why not?" I'd driven her truck before, even took it on the freeway, which was impressive since I never shifted out of second gear.

I came around to the door and paused. "Is it safe?"

"Fuck you. It's got a gas pedal, brakes, and a steering wheel. What more do you need?"

She was working full time at the garage now, covering the mortgage on her dad's place. I'd asked her a couple of days before if she'd mind giving me driving lessons.

I lowered myself into the driver's seat. The aged leather smelled like an old boat. The steering wheel was huge.

I tried to familiarize myself with the layout and clocked the stick shift. "Seriously?"

"My truck has a stick. Besides, you're going downhill this time."

"And that's good, because…?"

"Because it's easier. Look, are you gonna puss out, or drive?"

"One more question. "Where are we going?"

"Get us down the hill, and we'll see."

A few more people passed by as I studied the console.

I went over the checklist I'd learned back in high school. Radio - Off. Adjust the rearview mirrors. Secure the seatbelt and make sure the passengers secure their own - check.

I felt her amusement as I got ready. "Any Goddamn time, skippy," she said.

I stared down at the pedals.

"Jesus," she exclaimed. "You need to—"

"I know. I know." I said and stepped on the clutch, shoved the stick into first gear, released the parking brake, eased the clutch out, and gave it a little gas. The car lurched forward.

"Don't stop. Don't stop." Max laughed as she grabbed her cap before it blew off.

I stepped harder on the gas pedal and and we squealed around the driveway. I straightened it out and raced toward the exit.

"Easy. Easy!" she yelled.

I slammed on the brakes at the stop sign. The sudden stop threw us both forward.

"Oops."

She laughed. "You're doin' fine, speedy. Okay, look both ways."

It was my turn to give her a look.

She pointed forward. "The road's over there."

This time, I eased out into the street and turned left, trying to keep it smooth. Accelerating gradually, I shifted into second, and then third gear. "Bitchin," I whispered, surprised by my success.

"Nice. We're gonna get you laid yet."

The drive down the hill was much easier than I'd expected, with Max either encouraging or teasing me the entire way.

Roughly twenty minutes later, I pulled up in front of my house. The car bucked and died. "Sorry. Damn."

"What did we learn?" she asked.

I stared at the controls and guessed. "Put it in neutral?"

"...before shutting it down. Give the boy a gold star. What're you doing the rest of the day?"

"I might get together with Jessie."

"Cool. Alright, stud, out. I've got to get back to work."

I did and she settled in behind the steering wheel.

"Oh," she reached into the glove compartment grabbed something and handed it to me. It was a small booklet—The California Driver's Handbook.

"I didn't get you anything."

"Study it. Know it. You're taking the test next week."

"Next week?"

"You did good. Have fun tonight." She made a "V" with her fingers and wagged her tongue between them, then she started the car, and sped away.

The small gate clicked shut behind me and I saw Gram kneeling in the flower bed, wearing her floppy gardening hat, attacking the soil with a small spade. A haphazard pile of football-shaped leaves, branches, and huge violet, pink, and blue blossoms lay in a pile next to her.

"You pulled out the hydrangea?" The bush had dominated the space in front of our porch for as long as I could remember. It was a focal point of the yard. She'd doted on it. Its dried blossoms decorated half the rooms in our house.

She sat back on her haunches and regarded her work. "It was time for a change," she said.

The porch railing now stood stark and bare. It needed paint.

"Can I help?" I asked.

She shook her head. "I'm about done," she gathered what was left of the plant's remains and stuffed them into an old paint bucket.

I continued inside.

She entered as I was grabbing a Coke from the refrigerator, set her hat on the kitchen table and dropped the gloves inside.

"Was that you driving?" she asked.

"Max is teaching me."

"Snazzy car. How's she doing?"

Our last run-in with Lester had been a nightmare. He'd possessed Max's dad and forced him to beat a young girl to death, after which, he'd trapped us all in a house up in Boulder Creek and threatened to kill us and worse, trap our souls so he could feed on our torment for, well, eternity. Max had been forced to shoot her father in the head.

"She seems okay," I said.

"You know she's faking it, right?"

I didn't reply.

She patted my hand. "Just be her friend."

In the time since, Max had moved back into her father's house with her stepmother, Bunny. They used to hate each other, but apparently, that'd changed.

No one outside of our small group knew the real story about her dad. To the rest of the world, he was a cop gone bad. To us, he was a victim.

"Are you and Jessie going out tonight?"

I shook my head. "She's busy with something, and I've got homework." I held up the handbook.

Studying for my driver's permit test and my job at The Tattler took up the next few days. My boss, Mr. White had asked me to write a profile about a local businessman - an accountant, for God's sake. It was basically an expanded advertisement disguised as a human interest piece. The guy had paid for it, and was counting on us to make him seem trustworthy, and his profession exciting. I was pretty sure this was Mr. White's way of testing me, to see if I could pull it off, and I'd procrastinated for as long as I could.

I'd been at it for a couple of hours, but sitting on my bed, the longer I stared at my notes the more indecipherable they became. Scenes from the past few months competed for my attention, one would capture my focus just to be overtaken by another.

First, it's dusk and Max and I are riding in my little boat on the bay, completely unaware of the horror that awaits us. The next, we're fighting for our lives in the middle of a savage storm, rain pelting down as massive waves pummel us over and over again. Suddenly, I'm inside the lighthouse. It's pitch dark, and icy cold, and Max stares at me from a doorway with hatred burning hot in her eyes.

The words on the page could've been hieroglyphics for all the sense they made. Frustrated, I grabbed my coat and headed out into the night, hoping to organize my thoughts and clear my head.

So much had changed in just a few short months.

All my life, I'd been afraid of most everything: heights, bullies, girls - things that really couldn't hurt me. Now, I'd traded those things for real, deadly dangers.

I'd blamed myself for the stuff Max and I'd gone through, and sure, us being out on the water in that storm - that was on me.

But what Lester'd done; the murders, the possessions, Inspector Morales' death - that was on him.

My mind free-floated in this existential morass—an emotional soup—drifting from one thing to another, then they settled on Jessie, and how she'd entered my life so effortlessly, and in the few weeks since, had changed my life. I wouldn't have been so fired up to get my license or go back to school if it hadn't been for her.

Maybe one day, I'd be able to buy a car, live on my own—even get a degree. *Who was this guy?*

So overwhelmed was I with my thoughts that I snagged my toe on a raised bit of concrete. It sent me stumbling forward, wrenching me out of my reverie like a needle ripped off a vinyl record.

Confused and disoriented, I pivoted, trying to get my bearings. The window next to me was dark, save for a dim, flickering glow that backlit words painted on the glass: The Serpent's Eye.

What the hell was I doing here?

The little bell sounded loud and shrill in the closed quiet of the night, as the door swung open.

"Sam?"

It was Sylvia, dressed in a black hooded robe.

She stepped back, bidding me to enter.

It didn't occur to me to refuse. As I stepped over the threshold, the scene took on a dreamlike feel. The furniture had been pushed to the walls, with the huge red carpet rolled back to reveal the outline of a metal circle, inlaid into the hardwood floor, with arcane symbols hand-drawn inside. A candle set on a large stand burned on the edge, and in the center stood another robed figure.

"Hey there," said a familiar voice as she pushed back her hood and smiled.

"Jessie?"

9

MAGIC

HAVE YOU EVER WALKED IN UNEXPECTEDLY ON A conversation, and got the feeling they'd been talking about you? Standing there, with my mouth hanging wide open, I felt like that, self-conscious, but with an added, *how the hell did I end up here* vibe added to it. Oh, and there was the whole - witch-thing going on.

I was damned uncomfortable.

"Sam, would you turn on the light?" asked Sylvia.

I blinked and found the switch on the wall next to me.

The room brightened, revealing Jessie's face. It was flushed. Her eyes wide - excited. "I just cast my first spell."

"Really? What did you conjure?" I said, trying to get a better sense of the situation, and at the same time, sound supportive.

She practically bounded as she crossed the space between us and kissed me. "You. I conjured you."

"No, seriously, what's going on here?"

Sylvia moved the candle to the wall. "She's a natural. Could you two give me a hand?" She took her place behind the carpet roll. We joined her.

She placed her foot on top. We did likewise and we pushed. A few more kicks and it lay flat as it had before. I stood back as the two of them returned the furniture to it's original arrangement.

"Seriously," I repeated.

The two of them lifted a table loaded with incense and candles and other burnable things and sidestepped it to its place on the rug. "I-I've been learning some–" Jessie began.

Sylvia interjected. "I've been introducing her to the Craft."

"As in, witch-craft?"

Jessie jumped in. "Sam, it's like there's a completely different world, right here, alongside the one we know, with its own set of rules, and we can access it."

So, this is why she'd been so busy the last few days.

"Would you like some tea?" Without waiting for an answer, Sylvia disappeared. When I say disappeared, I mean she left the room the mundane way, by walking behind the counter into the back. She didn't de-materialize or anything. "I'll be out in a minute."

I took Jessie's hand. "You've been doing what, now?"

"I see that look. I'm not crazy."

"I didn't say you were crazy."

"Your eyes said I was crazy."

They should've communicated concern, suspicion. "Ignore them. They lie."

"Lyin' eyes?" She smiled.

"I love me some Eagles. So, about the, uh…" I pinched the fabric of her robe.

"Yeah, that. The other night kind of freaked me out. But I liked Sylvia. I got a good feeling from her. Anyway, I decided, rather than fear something I knew nothing about, maybe I should try to learn more about it. I came back here the next day."

"She's got a real knack," Sylvia yelled from the back. Bitchin'.

"And just now, you were—"

"Manifesting."

"Manifesting me?"

"Yep.

"I started just a few minutes before you walked in."

"But I was out walking for over an hour. How—?"

Sylvia entered, carrying a tray with a teapot and cups. "'How' doesn't enter into it." She set it down on the same table where she'd told my fortune, but lifted the dark fabric, folded it three times, and set it aside.

"What do you mean?"

"Magic can transcend the boundaries most people accept as concrete. Distance and time have little meaning in the Craft."

"Doesn't that seem a little convenient?"

"Convenient?"

"Yeah, if something's a coincidence, you could say it's magic, right? Why couldn't this be the place I was headed when I left my house?"

"Was it?" she asked with a smug smile.

I chose to not answer that question.

"How do you explain Sylvia finding us in the candle shop just as we were starting our fight?" Jessie asked, "Or how we found ourselves outside her store later that night?"

I held up my hands. "I'm not saying magic isn't real."

"It kinda sounds like you are."

Sylvia poured tea into the first cup. "Jessie, let him get a word in," she said patiently.

I took a breath to gather my thoughts. "Look, I don't want to seem disrespectful."

"Tea's ready," she said.

I whispered in Jessie's ear, "How much was the robe?"

"She didn't charge me," she whispered back.

A moment later, I was sitting with two women wearing witches' robes, drinking tea out of little fru-fru porcelain cups. This was weird, even for me.

Sylvia offered me a cookie. "If you let me, I'm sure I could change your mind about all this."

"No, thank you. I think I had enough reality the last time."

She winced. "Yeah, sorry about that. Things got a little…"

Disturbing? Frightening? Intrusive?

Jessie spoke up. "Sam, there's nothing to be nervous about. Please? For me?"

I've always been a pushover. It's something I should work on. I really didn't want to, but the way she looked at me… "Fine." I caved.

Sylvia set down her cup, reached across the table and took my hand, then said in a mellifluous tone (mellifluous —a five-dollar word I picked up from Mr. White), "Just listen to my voice. Let go of the world. Just be. That's it…" She went on like that for a while.

"Unclench your jaw. Let your shoulders drop. You're floating in the ether. A part of the cosmos. A universe within." Her voice soothed the inner chatter that always questioned my choices, warned me about things I thought I needed to fear. My worries fell away, and then it was just me being guided by her.

It felt as if she cradled my essence in her hand, and I surrendered to her, gave over the controls, and everything was better. Free of form or thought or concern, I drifted in diaphanous blackness with no sense of myself, safe and free and—

Hot pain seared my fingers, then blasted through my body like lightning.

I recognized the feeling that followed - the sudden disoriented shift in reality I'd first experienced in the Lighthouse, when Suzie, Lester Tod's dead daughter invaded my thoughts to show me what he'd done to her and her family.

This time the air was thick with the stink of rotted hay and pig shit. The stench forced its way into the back of my throat and lodged there.

Rusty tools lay scattered on a workbench and the ground. A pitchfork - its handle cracked and splintered - leaned against a wall.

I stood in a dilapidated barn.

The hog didn't fight me as I tied its legs to the corners of its stall. I didn't speak any soothing words or pet the beast to calm its nerves. It wasn't necessary. My father had long since beaten the spirit out of it.

I drew out the pocket knife I'd stolen years earlier from the feed and grain supply.

My hand quivered as I unfolded the blade and took my place behind the beast.

I held the knife still for a moment to steady my hand, then drew it slowly across the beast's back leg, just above the joint, where the meat thickened. The edge was dull, so it tore as much as it cut and the pig screamed and bucked at the sudden pain. Blood spurted onto my face. I tasted copper.

My ears rang with the piercing squeals as I worked my way around. Slicing here, stabbing there. I jabbed its eyes, first the right, then the left, then stood still, quiet, making it guess where the next attack would land.

It whimpered, shivering on its weakened legs.

I held my breath, drawing out the anticipation, The beast snorted. Its breath coming in quick, short gasps. I wanted to make this last, but I couldn't hold back anymore. I threw myself onto its back and stabbed over and over again, forcing my blade through its thick hide, deep into its flesh, scraping the bones beneath. It cried out, bucking and tearing at the ground, desperate to escape its fate. I struck again and again, covering its hide with jagged cuts. Blood spurted from countless wounds, and still I kept on, jabbing again and again, tearing at its ears with my teeth, Trying to wring every drop of blood and pain and terror as I could, Finally, exhausted from its fight and loss of blood, it collapsed - first one back leg, and then the other. Its breath came in ragged heaves. I reached under its head and sawed the knife across its throat. Its warm blood flowed over my hand.

Finally, with a wheeze, its miserable life was over. It lay still underneath me, blood dribbling out of its still carcass.

The world was a beautiful, peaceful hue of red, as I rested on its back.

"What have you done?" the voice slurred, loud and rough.

I lifted my head and saw my father.

He wore his best button-up shirt, the stained white fabric pulled tight across his belly. The gold clover-shaped pendant hanging below his throat glimmered in the moonlight shining through the caved ceiling. Funny, those four leaves had never brought him luck - not the good kind.

His fly gaped u.

I giggled as I got to my feet, tightening my grip on the knife.

He grabbed a hammer from the cluttered workbench, hefted it and shuffled toward me.

I stepped out of the stall and faced him, giving myself room to maneuver.

"You crazy little bastard." He pronounced it *bashtard.*

"That pig would've covered our rent for months. Let's see what your hide brings."

He rushed me, his face a mask of fury, his body a locomotive powered by liquor and rage.

Yes! I felt almost giddy. Hell, I *was* giddy. Two in one night!

I stepped lightly out of his way. He tried to correct, but his legs tangled underneath him and, screaming words I couldn't understand, he flopped down onto the dead hog.

This was going to be easy. Easier than the pig. I fought the urge to drop on top of him and finish him there and then. I wanted to enjoy this.

He staggered to his feet, and, snarling through his stained and crooked teeth, charged again, putting all his helpless rage and hopelessness into his attack. Again, I waited until the last moment, then pivoted. In my head, I danced like one of those Spanish bullfighters.

As he passed, I lashed out with my blade, ripping through his shirt and tearing a line in his side.

He twisted in pain and went down again. If he was smart, he'd give up. Escape. Sleep it off, so he could take it out on me in the morning. He wasn't.

I'd never stood up to my father before. I'd swallowed my disgust. Hid my anger. I'd used animals: stray cats, dogs, and whatever else I could catch to control my anger, to quiet my need to dominate, torture, kill.

The pig's blood, growing cold and sticky, tightened on my skin. I could still taste it. I was hungry for more.

"No way you're my kid," he said, struggling to his feet. "Stringy and weak."

I feinted with the knife.

He flinched, then swung the hammer. I felt the wind as it whipped past my face.

Shouting something I couldn't understand, he spread

his arms and bowled down on me. There wasn't room to dodge, so I backpedaled.

I tripped and went down. The pig cushioned my fall.

My old man charged on, thinking he had me.

I waited, watching him come. At the last instant, I kicked his shin. He cried as his foot flew out from under him, pitching him forward. I rolled out of his way, and he landed face down on his pig.

I stuck again - this time in the kidney.

He arched his back and grunted.

Rolling to my feet, I crouched in the stall's opening, ready for his next attack.

He struggled back to his feet and shuffled toward me. "You'll be fertilizing next year's crop for that." He rasped from between clenched teeth.

What crop? He hadn't planted anything in years.

I smiled. This was a lot more fun than killing pigs.

He swung the hammer hard, putting all his strength into the blow.

This time, rather than dodge, I ducked under his swing and plunged my blade deep into his gut.

"Oh!" His look was at the same time, surprised and ridiculous.

I held tight to the knife as he slid off it and collapsed to the ground. His shirt was now more red than white.

I stepped on his wrist, snatched the hammer from his broken grip, hefted it once, then brought it down hard on his forearm.

The bones made a satisfying crack. He moaned and turned onto his side.

I kicked him back over.

His gold charm gleamed in the moonlight. It was his last thing of value—a wedding gift from my mother, before he'd broken her, like he broke everything. Except me.

I climbed on top of him, trapping his arms beneath my knees. I grasped the chain and tried to yank it off, like I'd seen in the movies, but it wouldn't snap. He gagged as I twisted it, trying to break the clasp. His hand, the one that still worked, waved feebly in the air.

I raised the blade and smiling, got to work, sawing through skin and sinew, and bone. The little blade was a poor tool for this job. I leaned into the challenge.

I didn't notice when he stopped fighting. I didn't notice when he stopped breathing. I remained focused on my goal.

When I was done, the bloody husk that'd been my father lay in pieces next to the pig. In my hand, I held the one thing he valued.

With his blood still dripping off it, I took my golden prize and headed to the house to clean up, leaving this mess for the flies.

Tomorrow, I'd be gone.

———

The jolt shot through me, sending me flying backward through the air.

Someone screamed.

Something crashed hard into my lower back, stopping my and came to rest on the floor as small objects rained down around me.

I struggled to breathe, my lungs rejected the air before I could fill them.

"Sam!"

I wheezed as I fought for air.

"You're okay. Please be okay." It was Jessie! She grasped my hand. Her face mirrored the panic I felt.

She caressed my face. "C'mon. Shallow breaths. That's it. I think you got the wind knocked out of you."

She knelt next to me, coaching me to relax so I could

breathe. Finally, air seeped in, just a little. With each gasp my lungs opened a little wider. Unclenched a bit more.

What just happened?

I pushed out the whisper. "Sylvia?"

"Shit." She gently released my hand, whispering, "I'll be right back." She hurried away. "Sylvia?"

I forced my way to my knees. Shards tumbled off me to join broken ceramic statuettes covering the ground. Steadying myself on the table I'd crashed into, I pulled myself to my feet. Sylvia lay trembling on the carpet, with Jessie bent over her.

Tears streamed down the sides of Sylvia's face. "It-it was all right there. So clear; Suzie, little Elisabeth, ... Lester, his father. I didn't know."

Confusion, anger, fear - yeah, I felt all that, but mostly I felt betrayed.

"Sam..." Jessie began.

Violated again. Someone had pushed their way inside me and taken something. This was too much.

I stared at them - my girlfriend, and her, what - mentor? Both wearing matching robes, and me standing apart. Alone, again.

"You had no right," I whispered.

Sylvia's searching eyes found me. "I'm so sorry."

"Fuck your *sorry*." Without another word, I lurched toward the door and limped out into the night.

10

THE TATTLER

STILL REELING FROM THE NIGHT BEFORE, I SAT IN THE kitchen, hunched over a cup of coffee with cream and lots of sugar. My body ached from whatever it was that'd happened and the long walk home afterward.

My heart stung.

Were Jessie and I done? How could I trust her again? I kicked myself for going against my instincts with Sylvia. How the hell had she dragged Lester's visions out of my head—visions I'd never seen before.

The phone rang. I let the machine answer. "Hi Sam, This is Mr. White. I just wanted to know if you planned to come in today. I've got something important…" I missed the rest of the message as I rushed through the house. He hung up just as I picked up the handset.

I dialed his number. "Mr. White? Sorry, I slept through my alarm. Yeah, I should be there in a half hour. The profile?" Shit. "Of course. See you then."

I dashed into my room, scribbled something on a piece of paper, then threw some clothes on and ran out the door.

I was late.

He was in his office, standing behind a table, staring at a large piece of cardboard. The Tattler's masthead was pinned to the top. Beneath it lay a headline: "Eighth Woman Found Beaten to Death - 'No Leads,' say police."

The headline took me back to the night Lester killed Christine Dunn, a cheerleader at my old high school. I'd experienced her murder in a vision, as if he'd attacked me. Suddenly, I was back in that parking lot, battered. Terrified. I felt the rough asphalt beneath my face, smelled his rancid cigar breath.

"Just the man I wanted to see." He walked me out to the bullpen, which was a room filled with old, wooden desks - unoccupied. He guided me to one and sat me down. Here's a list of local businesses. Here's a script. Dial the numbers, read the script."

I glanced at it, then looked back up at him.

"You look confused."

I was.

"Mr. Fremen, how do you think this business survives?"

I hadn't really thought about it.

"The Tattler's a free paper. No one ever pays for a copy. Advertising my boy covers the rent, the paper, ink, your wages, my wages. I could do it, but then who'd put the paper together?" He pointed again to the desk. "Call the names. Read the script. Comprende?

I nodded.

"Good. Oh, do you have that piece for me?"

I reached into my pocked and pulled out the wadded sheet of paper I'd scribbled on.

He didn't bother to read it. He simply exhaled his impatience and tapped the desk with his finger. "Call. Read."

11

SOMETHING'S WRONG

I GOT HOME LATER THAT AFTERNOON. GETTING THE PHONE slammed in my ear countless times had done nothing to improve my mood.

Gram wasn't home so I headed into my room, figuring I should finally crack open the Driver's Ed booklet.

I'd just settled onto my bed when the front door opened and Gram's soft footsteps padded into the house. I listened to her set down her purse and keys and then move into the kitchen. She opened the cupboard, then the freezer—which she slammed shut—then dropped ice into a glass. A moment later, she stood at my door, whisky in hand.

"You're home." I said.

"Studying?" She sipped.

"Just started. Where were—?" My question was cut short as she wandered off toward her room. She simply turned and shuffled off down the hall as if I hadn't been saying a thing.

I put the book down and followed. What I saw would've been comical if it hadn't been so bizarre—like watching a clown car accident in slow motion. I arrived at her door as she, while holding her drink in one hand, tried to lift her dress over her head with the other. She got lost in loose fabric as it wound around her, splashing whisky onto the shag carpet. She paused with her head lost in a curtain of flowered cotton.

"Can I help?"I asked.

"I'm fine," she shot back.

The hell she was. I took her arm to free it from the sleeve.

She snatched it back. "Leave me the fuck alone," she snapped.

"I'm sorry. I'll uh—"

"Get out!"

"Sorry," I repeated. Feeling like a whipped dog, I slunk into my room.

Jessie called later. By that time, Gram was sleeping; passed out really, on her bed. I dragged the phone into my room and closed the door, and said softly, "Hello?"

"Sam, it's me. I wanted to say... Are you whispering?" Jessie asked.

"I guess. What's up?" For the first time, I wasn't stoked that she called. The sound of her voice left me feeling cold. Maybe I didn't have the energy to spare, what with Gram acting strange again. Or, maybe after last night, I was over her.

"As I was saying, ..." She stopped herself again. "You are whispering. Is it Gram?"

Her damned intuition. I held my tongue. I hated feeling like this, like I'd shut down inside.

"Sam, talk to me. What's going on?"

"Nothing. I'm - everything's fine."

"No, it's not. I can hear it in your voice."

I didn't want to open up. Last night was still too fresh

in my mind. "Look, I uh, I gotta go." I hung up. I didn't have the will to put any effort into being nice or accommodating. My emotions had switched off. After last night, I didn't owe her anything, and I definitely didn't want her help.

I could apologize later. Maybe.

Suddenly, the book didn't interest me either. I set it back on my nightstand.

A little later, I heard a soft knock on our door. I opened it, and there stood Jessie holding a pair of ice cream cones —obviously from Penny's. Nobody over-packs a cone like Penny's. She held one out for me, with two scoops: mint chip and bing cherry, of course. God knows how she drove with them. "Truce?" Her eyes were puffy and red. Had she been crying? Over me?

Seeing her like that melted whatever ice had formed around my heart. I accepted her offering, and we fell into each other's arms. It was that simple.

"I'm so sorry," she began.

"Don't," I said.

"Really, I didn't realize—"

"Seriously. Stop." I didn't want to ruin things by talking about it.

She must have picked up on my not-so-subtle vibe and after kissing and holding each other for a while, she pivoted. "What's going on with Gram?"

I sighed. The reunion had been so pleasant. "She came home drunk."

"Drunk?" She scoffed.

I didn't see the humor. "I don't know what to do."

"Sorry. It's just, that doesn't sound like her."

"She didn't act like her."

"Any idea what's going on? What's she doing now?"

"She's sleeping, and I'm afraid to say."

"Say it anyway."

An idea had occurred to me, but I was afraid to speak it out loud, for fear it would give it weight.

"Lester?" she whispered timidly, as if the name alone had power.

Shit. She was thinking it, too.

"I don't have any proof or anything," I said. "She might just be going through a thing…"

"Yeah." Jessie was quiet for a moment. "So, how do we find out?"

"I don't know. I can't ask her."

"Oh, that'd go well." She went silent again, not looking at me.

"You're thinking."

"I'm stalling. You're not gonna like my suggestion."

She wanted me to call Sylvia.

"No."

"Sylvia felt awful—"

"How do you think I felt, walking home with a cracked rib, after someone else had kicked their way into my head?"

"You cracked a rib?"

"Maybe. I could have."

"She didn't mean to."

"Look, you want to hang out with her, doing whatever. Fine. Enjoy yourself. I don't trust her."

There, I'd laid my cards on the table. We stood awkwardly, looking at each other. "Maybe I'm worrying about nothing," I blurted. "Maybe she just wanted a drink and got carried away."

Jessie started sheepishly. "Has she ever done this before?"

"No. Still, it doesn't mean she's… you know, possessed, right?"

"Right. Sure."

"I mean, maybe she's stressed or something and just wanted to take the edge off."

"Sure. Right."

"It was just an innocent drink, after all. People do it all the time."

"All the time."

"Are you mocking me? I asked. I felt cold liquid dripping down my knuckles. The ice cream was melting.

"What do you want me to say? The only person we know with any experience—"

"Besides us."

"Yes, besides us, is Sylvia."

"Do we actually know she has experience with ghosts, spirits—whatever? All we know is, she's a witch."

"You don't have to say it like that."

I didn't mean it in a good way. "I appreciate your support - really. I just..." I needed to talk with someone else who had experience with the supernatural, who knew Gram well enough to tell me if I was crazy or not. Someone I could trust.

With Jessie following, I made a beeline for the phone, dragged it into my room, and dialed.

"Hey, Max?"

"Hey, what's up? Get laid yet?"

I paused, trying to form the words in my head. "Listen, when your dad was...you know, possessed, how did he act?"

"I'm coming over."

A few minutes later, Max walked through the door. She didn't need to knock. Family doesn't knock.

I led her into the kitchen and together, Jessie and I filled her in on the events of the past few days.

"That doesn't sound like Gram."

Jessie smiled. "That's what I said."

"Can we not?" I said.

"I don't know," Max began. "If that asshole's back, why hasn't he attacked us directly? Why Gram?"

"Why your dad?"

She ticked the reasons off on her fingers. "Because he had a gun. He was a cop."

"What better way to get to us than through Gram?" Jessie said. "I hate to push, but did he act any different?"

She shrugged. "Hard to say. I hardly saw him."

"So, no change? Nothing?" I was floundering.

Max shook her head slowly. "Were there any signs? Should I have known something was up? I keep asking myself." She shrugged.

"Was he drinking?"

She shrugged. "Maybe? There was a vibe, an edge, maybe, but..." She shrugged then looked me in the eye.

"You think I should talk to Sylvia."

"After what you told me, it sounds like maybe she's for real. Otherwise, I don't know. A priest?"

"Gram hates priests."

"Really? Why?"

I shrugged. "No idea."

"Then Witchiepoo it is."

"Crap."

Jessie spoke up. "On the bright side, maybe this is just a mild case of alcohol poisoning or something."

"Cheery," I swallowed my pride and after looking up the number in the Yellow Pages, got her on the phone. Max and Jessie stood close. I angled the handset so they could listen.

"Sam, I'm glad you called. I really want to apologize—"

I didn't care. I interrupted, and told her about Gram. "How do we know if she really is possessed?" I asked.

"Is she still sleeping?"

"Yeah, I think so."

"Can you go into her room without waking her up?"

"Probably. She passed out pretty hard."

"Okay, without disturbing her, see if she's wearing the necklace."

"What necklace? Lester's necklace? The clover? How would she get it?"

"Don't worry about that. If she has it, you'll know for sure. But Sam…"

"Yeah?"

"Whatever you do, don't touch it."

"Okay, but why?"

"Just promise me, whatever you do, don't let it touch your skin."

"Got it."

"I'm on it," said Max already heading to Gram's room, her boots thudding down the hall, with Jessie on her heels.

"Quietly," I whisper-shouted, then set down the phone and followed.

Max paused at the door. "If she wakes up, I'm gonna have some big explaining to do," she whispered, then approached as quietly as she could.

Gram lay under the light blanket I'd thrown over her earlier, soft snores gurgled from her throat.

Jessie and I crowded the doorway, holding our breath, as Max reached down toward the blanket's edge. Her hand hovered just an inch or so above it, then her fingertips pinched the fabric and lifted it slowly. We all saw the golden gossamer chain on her neck. Max raised the blanket higher until she could confirm it was Lester's charm.

"See something you like?" Gram's voice froze my heart.

Max jumped as if she'd been burned.

Gram's eyes shot to me. I recognized Lester's squint. "How 'bout you, li'l Kipper? Wanna see granny's tits?"

She lifted her head.

"Hold her," Jessie yelled.

I rushed past Max, leapt onto the bed, grabbed Gram's arms, and pinned them to the mattress.

Her smile broadened. "Eager boy." The expression, the voice - it was a mockery of Gram's, but gravelly, with a cruel, smug tone. Her features had twisted, adopting Lester's pinched eyes and joyless smile.

"I'll find some rope," Max said, and hurried off.

Jessie got to the foot of the bed and took hold of Gram's ankles.

Gram's back arched, raising her chest toward me. "Come on, Kip. Let's have it out."

She bucked savagely. The bed tipped to one side, its legs lifting off the floor, then slammed back down again. It rolled one way then the other, like a boat on a wicked sea.

I wasn't letting go, but how long could I hold on before she'd hurl me across the room?

Max returned with a coil of white cord. "It was in your garage."

"Great! Help me turn her over."

The bed froze. Gram's expression changed from mocking to furious. She lifted her face toward me. "Behave, boy, or I'll switch her off." Her head dropped onto the bed, mouth agape, her eyes staring at nothing. No movement. No breath.

I froze.

A minute passed without a twitch. I placed my ear on her chest. There was no breath or heartbeat.

"She never did anything to you!" I screamed. "Get out!" I lost myself, spitting words and saliva, punching the bed in impotent fury.

I'd had it. I was done. I'd always said I didn't believe in violence. That's what made me better than the assholes who tormented me when I was younger. But the truth was, I'd been afraid. I was scared of what they'd do to me if I fought back.

When you lose control, you don't do it consciously. You don't surrender. It's snatched away like a magician's table-cloth. One minute, you're raging at the injustice of life— the unfairness of the world—and the next, you're punching your grandmother in the face.

I struck hard, slamming the smug son of a bitch in the face, just below the eye. I pulled back to strike again.

I couldn't. My fist was held in place. Max stood next to me, trapping my arm with her own.

She shoved me backward. I reeled, tripped over the foot of the bed, and landed on my head. Gram's room was carpeted in thick, green shag. I wasn't hurt, but Max had stopped me. I jumped to my feet.

She squared off in a fighting stance, her fists cocked and ready. I'd seen this pose before, but never as the intended target.

I held up my hands. "Thank you." I meant it.

Gram reached up to her reddening cheek. "Nice punch, Kip."

At least I hadn't killed her.

She smiled, Lester's mealy worm-ridden smile. "Let me go, and maybe she'll live - for however long. She ain't got much left." There was that smile again.

"Or I end her now."

He held up an arthritic, bony fist. It seemed so frail. Thick blue veins bulged underneath the webbed skin. Her face looked drawn, the skin lifeless and gray. Was she really that old? "Deal's going once." He raised a finger.

"Twice." Two fingers.

"Fine," Max said softly, still facing me.

"Great." He sat up slowly, then swung Gram's legs over the side of the bed.

"We can't lose her too," Max whispered.

I wanted to grab her, to hold her there and prevent her from leaving. But Max held me back in an embrace that was just firm enough to keep me in place.

Jessie blocked the door. "Jessie, let her go," Max said.

She stepped toward us, clearing the way.

Max held tight, as Lester stuffed Gram's feet into her shoes and shuffled out the door, into the hallway, and without looking back, raised her right hand and flipped us off.

Max didn't let go as we stood in that room that smelled of lilac and Gram, each of us lost in despair. She no longer restrained me. We held each other, seeking solace as we listened to Lester pick up Gram's purse and keys from the dining room table, open the door, and then close it behind.

Only then, when she was sure Gram had gone, Max began to tremble. Resting her head on my shoulder, together, we wept.

12

LESTER

"I don't get why he didn't go after each of us. Before, he hopped from one body to the next like a kid playing hopscotch." Jessie said. We'd gathered in *The Serpent's Eye*. Sylvia had flipped the closed sign and locked the door.

"He's attached to that necklace now. It needs to be touching someone's skin for him to control them," she said as she emerged from the back room carrying a tray with tea and cookies.

I didn't want any fucking cookies. "But, how did he get her to put it on? Shouldn't it still be in the police station or something?"

Sylvia, in the middle of pouring, fumbled, spilling tea on the tray and counter. Jessie rushed over to help.

"Something you'd like to add?" Max had been eyeing Sylvia since we'd arrived.

"Sorry. Just clumsy."

"I was touching Gram. I held her by her wrists. That's skin to skin contact. Why didn't he jump into me?"

"Because it doesn't work that way. You need to be in direct contact with the object itself. Period."

"And how was he able to fool me? When he possessed Max at the lighthouse, I knew there was something wrong right away."

"Because he can. Look, you've got to stop asking *how* or *why*. It won't change anything. The fact is, he's leashed to that charm. He can't leave it, but once it makes contact with someone, the connection is more intense than what he was capable of before. It's spiritual and physical. He's able to act like her, because he's controlling her, not just her body."

Max grabbed a cookie. "How are you so sure?"

"What do you mean?" Sylvia paused in her cleaning.

"I mean, how do you know? Where does this knowledge come from?"

She straightened. "I've been dealing with this sort of thin for a long time."

"This sort of thing?" Max scoffed. "I don't think so. I doubt anybody deals with this sort of thing. You might host an occasional seance or something, but I can't imagine that this sort of thing happens all the time."

"Oh, you'd be surprised," said Sylvia. She went back to her cleaning.

"Really? Surprise me." Max bit into the cookie.

"What're you getting at?" Jessie asked.

"I'm saying it's pretty convenient that a witch materializes right when we need her, almost like she knew it was coming. And she's willing to help for free." She swallowed, then cleared her throat. "Cookies are dry, by the way." She tossed the remnants back onto the tray.

"What exactly are you accusing me of?" Sylvia stood up straight, wringing her towel in her hands.

Max continued. "If you're into this because you think

there'll be some sort of reward, I've got news for you - we got nothing. If you're hoping for... I don't know, publicity or something, okay, I get that, you've got a business to run. But if you claim you're helping us out of the goodness of your heart, I call bullshit."

"Why?" Jessie asked.

"Because people - especially business people - aren't built that way. There's something in it for her, and I want to know what it is."

"Sam, are you hearing this?" Jessie looked distressed.

Max was onto something. I simply nodded.

"After everything she's done?" Jessie stood up. Incensed.

"Especially after what she's done," I said.

"I can't believe this. You realize I'm your best chance to save your gram, right?" Sylvia folded her arms in front of her.

"Maybe." Max said. "My dad taught me to be suspicious of folks doing things 'just to be nice'."

"Your dad the policeman? Sounds like a lonely way of living." She turned her attention to me. Sam, why do you think I'm trying to help?"

A single word screamed in my head, like a flash of intuition. "Guilt."

Judging by her face, if she'd have been holding the teapot, she'd have dropped it again.

"G-guilt? Guilty of what?" Her arms dropped to her sides.

"You tell me." I continued. I didn't know where I was going, but I decided to follow my instinct. "Something's been eating at me. Last night I lived through a scene from Lester's past. I thought maybe I'd covered it up or something. God knows It was fucking horrible enough. But, what if it wasn't my memory? What if it was something

Lester planted in your head?" I was on a roll. I didn't pause to consider, I just let the words flow.

"What if - and again, I'm just thinking out loud - what if it's your fault that my grandmother is walking the streets with a fucking sadistic serial killer inside her?"

Jessie stepped forward. "Sam, that's crazy. She's been nothing but helpful. Where is this coming from?"

Something about Sylvia had bothered me since we met. That Max sensed it too, cemented my suspicion that something wasn't right.

Tension built in the silent room as we stared at each other, unblinking. A still frame painted on glass bending at the edges, threatening to shatter.

"Seriously...!" Jessie began.

Sylvia silenced her with a gesture. Her veneer cracked, and she broke eye contact. "Shit."

Slowly, she crossed to the wall where the pewter statuettes were displayed, and knelt. Below the open shelves was a cupboard. She opened it and drew out something wrapped in black fabric, then returned cradling it like a baby. "A member of my coven works in the police department. She rescued this from the evidence locker." She peeled back the cloth, revealing a black ceramic burial urn.

"What the fuck?" Max looked like she was ready to throw Sylvia to the ground.

"They asked me to keep it safe." She laid it down on the table, almost tenderly. "There was so much power, I couldn't resist." With nothing to hold, her hands kneaded together. "I thought I could control..." She wiped a tear from her cheek. "He made me search out your gram. He knew her habits from when he'd taken her over before. It-it was simple. I bumped into her outside the grocery store and dropped the charm into her hand."

Max whispered. "Do you know what you've done?"

"H-he showed me what he'd do to me if I tried to warn you. I was sure he'd come find me either way. It's not like him to leave loose ends. So, I tried to help from a distance."

Jessie stepped forward. "The candle shop?"

"I recognized you two from his memories, and that gave me an opening."

"How long?" I asked.

"What?"

"How long has he been controlling her?"

"Two weeks."

My thoughts ran back over that time, seeing Gram's change. "He could've murdered me in my sleep."

"It was hell for him, isolated in there. No one to reach out to. To feed on."

"There's no telling how many people he's hurt since then," Max said.

"Eight," I replied.

"Eight what?"

"Eight people. Girls. Beaten to death. I saw the headline."

"Gram? But how…?" Jessie's voice trailed off.

"You saw how strong he was," I said. "An old lady riding the bus around town. Who'd suspect?"

Sylvia looked aghast. "You don't think I'm responsible…"

"You fucking think?" Max pushed the table over., sending the china tea service crashing to the floor. She grabbed Sylvia's shirt and pulled her face close. Their noses touched. "You're going to tell us every goddamned thing. What's his plan? Where can we find her? How do we stop him? Why the hell shouldn't I twist your head off your scrawny little neck?"

Filled with terror, Sylvia's eyes darted around the room. "Now!" Max screamed.

Jessie screamed. "But she didn't mean for any of this to happen."

Sylvia locked eyes with Max. "H-he's going to make Sam kill all of you." Her gaze shifted to me. "Everyone you love. Then he'll kill you too."

"And he wants to trap your souls, so he has something to play with.

"We know the Goddamned drill." Max shook her." Where is he? How can we stop him? Why didn't he kill you?"

"I don't know."

"Bullshit, lady. He was in your fucking head. He couldn't hide his plans from you. He wouldn't have tried. That's not his style. I fucking know."

"He-he wanted to get back to the lighthouse."

Max wasn't buying it. "He hated it there."

"I'm not sure why. He either left something, or... I don't know. His greatest weakness is the place where he's strongest."

"What is that? What do you mean?" I asked.

"I don't know. Just something that's been playing in my head."

"Is that a message or something?" Jessie asked.

"What's 'the place where he's strongest'?" Max asked.

Jessie spoke up. "Obviously, it's the lighthouse."

Max released Sylvia with a shove. "Maybe. But how is he strongest there?"

"It's a trap." I said. "Sylvia, so help me, if this is bullshit..."

"I think he's there," she said.

Max scanned the room. "You've got all this occult crap here. Is there a pendant, or wand, or ring, or something that can turn him into a vegetarian meatloaf or gerbil, or something?"

Sylvia folded her arms in front of of her, looking resigned. Defeated. "Most of this stuff is junk - for tourists."

Jessie spoke up. "Maybe we could manifest him here, but add a binding spell or something?"

Sylvia shook her head. "It won't work. Not like that."

"I don't understand," I said. "Two days ago you threw me across the room - by accident."

"I don't know what that was. I'm not even sure it was magic. It could've been some kind of psychic discharge or something."

Terrific.

"What about this?" Max pointed at a display case next to her. Inside was an intricately carved shaft of dark wood, about the size of a baseball bat.

Jessie spoke up. "She told me about that. It's a scepter - for the queen witch or something."

"The High priestess, but it doesn't have any power. It's ceremonial."

"You told me power is a result of belief and will," Jessie said.

"So, if you believe that something has power, it does?" I asked.

"Like money?" Max asked.

"There's a little more to it. Look, don't you think if there was anything that would work, I'd have tried it?"

Max shot her a look that would've melted steel. "Depends on what side you're on."

"It's the same problem as before." I said. "You can't kill a ghost. We really need to go,"

"Should we bring her?" Jessie asked.

"Why the fuck would we do that?" Max replied.

"Jessie, you stay here, too."

"Here, why?" She looked hurt.

"It's going to get rough." I said. "I won't be able to protect you."

"It's gonna suck balls," Max said. "You don't want any part of this."

Jessie crossed to the case, opened it, and lifted out the scepter. She hefted the weight like a club. "I care about Gram too, remember? Face it, I'm already part of it."

"What's that for?" Max asked.

"What could it hurt?" she replied.

13

RETURN TO THE LIGHTHOUSE

AFTER STOPPING AT MAX'S HOUSE FOR SUPPLIES, WE PULLED into the marina parking lot.

We were quiet. Each of us lost in our own thoughts I suppose, as we walked down to the dock and made for my boat, just a little fourteen foot aluminum skiff that'd belonged to my Grandpa. My fondest memories of him were the times we'd spent together on the water, catching fish, or just talking. It was so small, it didn't need its own slip.

"Damn!" I said.

"Fuck me!" Max echoed.

We stood at the base of the ramp, where it'd been berthed for years, staring at the empty cleats.

In the space where it usually floated was nothing but water. It was gone.

"What's wrong?" Jessie asked.

"That fucking asshole stole Sam's boat."

"Well, we know where to find it," I said, and marched out onto the docks.

Jessie hurried to catch up. "Where are you going?"

"To get it back." I headed for the largest, most beautiful yacht in the harbor. A real sailing vessel, so clean it almost glowed in the dark.

"Fuckin'-a," Max said, and immediately started untying the lines.

I jumped in and made for the captain's wheel.

Jessie called from the slip, "What's going on? Whose boat is this?"

I searched for the key. "The night we met, remember the douchebag who gave you a bad time?"

"Mitch Kavenaugh. You told me about him."

I found the key in the cupholder just as I had before, and held it up. Attached to it was a yellow floatation device that read *Sailors get you wetter.* "Alright Max, cast us off."

Jessie stepped over the rail and onto the deck. "This is his?"

"Something like that." I started the engine as Max threw the lines into the boat, pushed us out of the slip, then jumped aboard.

She hummed with confident power. I let us drift backward, and then eased the throttle forward, and pointed us out of the harbor.

Inside, my guts were in turmoil, like the storm that'd first wrecked my boat just a couple of months before, and set all of this in motion. All we had on our side was the hope that somehow things wouldn't totally go to shit. That's a hell of a thing to bet my friends' lives on, let alone my gram's.

If Sylvia was telling the truth, Lester'd been feeding off Gram for weeks now. What's worse, he could show you—no, worse—he could make you live through anything he wanted; images of him torturing us, killing me, visions of past crimes, etcetera... An unending violation of her soul, ripped open and shredded, with no chance to escape, not even in dreams, since he didn't have to sleep.

He was like some supernatural cockroach. We had to do more than beat him this time. Somehow, we needed to end him.

No other boats were out at play this late at night, which was normal. Over the years, I'd passed it countless times as we fished the bay, and always thought it ugly. With its squat tower hunched over the dilapidated living quarters, it looked like a cancerous growth that should've been amputated long ago. Now, I liked it even less.

The island itself was a jagged zit, jutting from the mouth of the bay, roughly a couple hundred feet high, and just wide enough to accommodate the crumbling building perched on top. Gliding over glassy water, we arrived quickly, and as we pulled in close to the rock, I set the motor to idle and let us coast.

The rock sloped out at the foot, forming a small, hazardous beachhead–the only possible place for a landing.

We drifted until the hull scraped, rough and hollow, on the rock below. "Unless you want to swim, this is where you two get off."

Max grabbed her pack and jumped, splash landing in ankle-deep water. She staggered a few steps, but kept her feet. Jessie tossed the scepter to her and accepted a hand down.

For safety, I took the yacht a little ways out, and dropped the anchor, then I made my way to the stern and stepped down onto the swim platform. It was going to be cold, but there was nothing I could do about that, so, steeling myself as best I could, I took a deep breath and dove in.

I'd done this before, but it wasn't something you get

used to. My body tried to contract into itself as the icy water stole my breath. Using short, quick strokes, I swam toward my friends, and, shivering violently, pulled myself up onto the slippery landing.

I spotted my little boat laying on the rock about halfway up the landing. Seeing it abandoned, leaning awkwardly to one side, separated from its aquatic environment hit me in a way that's difficult to describe. I've never had a pet, but Max used to have a dog - a little fluffy thing that yipped constantly. I remember how hard she cried when little Maya died. I'm not saying this was the same, but in a lot of ways I felt more at home in front of the tiller than I ever had on land. It was the most solid connection I still had to my Grandfather.

I fought the urge to check its condition. Gram was the priority, so, I took the lead, and headed toward the uneven staircase cut into the rock almost a century before. Max, shouldering her pack, brought up the rear.

Twin metal rails ran up the climb on either side. "Hang onto the railing," I said to Jessie. "It gets a little treacherous." I didn't pause to consider the weight of our mission, or to catch my breath; I simply stepped onto the first rise, and, using both rails to help pull me along, didn't stop until we'd reached the top.

Legs burning, we stepped out onto the apex, the man-made flat-top upon which the lighthouse perched. It was off to our left, taking up most of the area. Otherwise, the sky and the mirror sea were unobstructed. An ocean of stars above and below.

As before, it felt like I stood in the center of creation, and just like the last time, I had more immediate concerns.

"Okay, here you go." Max pulled flashlights from her pack and handed them out. Cheap plastic ones for us, while she hefted what looked like a metal club with a light on the end - a standard police-issue, Kel-Lite. Then she pulled on a pair of latex gloves.

I eyed the gloves. "For the necklace? Smart."

She then pulled one additional thing out of her pack. A gun - her dad's revolver. She flicked open the chamber, then flicked it closed again and held it out for me.

My stomach clenched. "No."

"We know this is a fucking trap," she said.

I shrugged. "Okay."

"He's had two weeks. God knows what he's got waiting for us," she said.

I argued. "The newspaper said the girls were beaten to death. There was no mention of a gun."

"It doesn't matter." She said. Her tone emphatic. "You can't ask me to fucking do it again."

"She's my family." I regretted saying it the instant the words left my mouth.

"So am I." She looked wounded.

"I'll trade you." Jessie stepped forward, holding out the scepter.

"Can we just lose the gun?" I really wished she hadn't brought it.

"I fucking hope it doesn't come to this, but it has to stop here. We can't let him leave this fucking island." Max turned to Jessie. "You ever fired one?"

Jessie shook her head.

Max sighed. "It's pretty simple. Just aim and shoot. The trigger's pretty hard to pull, so it probably won't go off accidentally. Still, don't point it at anything unless…"

"Where's the safety?"

"There isn't one."

Jessie handed the staff to Max and took the gun. "It's heavy."

"Please, just don't hurt anyone," I said.

We approached the door, beaten by decades and weather. It wasn't latched. I pushed, and it swung open slowly, squealing as the ancient hinges announced our arrival.

Inside, it looked exactly as I remembered. Deep cracks lined the walls, wooden lath showed through in the ceiling where the plaster had crumbled away and now lay scattered on the floor, but it was the smell, the musty damp odor of rot and age, that triggered my fear. I shuddered, then swallowed it. I needed to focus.

The room was empty.

Max and I stepped inside. My light showed that the room still held signs of our struggle; smeared blood, mostly mine, stained the floor from my first experience here, when Lester had used Max to try to kill me. He'd have succeeded if his daughter Suzie hadn't helped me.

Over my shoulder, I asked Jessie, "Are you okay?" This was some heavy shit we were facing. I'd have preferred for her to've stayed on the dock.

Our footsteps crackled as we crushed shards of plaster beneath our feet. Unable to see the entire room at once, our reality was limited to a shifting, confusing juggle of illuminated circles projected from the flashlights that moved with a flick of our wrists.

We weren't alone, and this time we knew it. Lester was here, wearing the flesh of my grandmother while he fed on her essence and tormented her soul. I'd pushed my fear aside, except for where she was concerned. For her, I was truly afraid. My hatred for him, on the other hand, had grown white hot.

We didn't need to speak. Max and I knew the layout of this place intimately. We stood next to each other while Jessie took up the rear.

We exited the main room and entered the rotunda.

The old iron staircase climbed along the graffiti-covered wall toward the lantern room above. At our feet, a thick, uneven line formed a circle. It arched around the room, and was inscribed with carelessly painted runes.

"Shhhh." Jessie grasped our shoulders.

"Did you hear something?" I whispered.

She simply squeezed, urging me to keep quiet. We stood completely still. My heartbeat drummed in my ears as I strained to sense whatever it was she'd heard.

Max crept forward. I felt Jessie pull her back.

We stood for a moment longer. Then... something. It may have been just a shifting of the breeze blowing through the open door behind us. Perhaps a whisper of rustled fabric, upset by the most subtle movement, or the change in pressure you experience in a room when someone else enters.

Whatever it was, I jerked my flashlight around to the left, toward the doorway that led to the old kitchen. There, on the lone chair, with her elbows resting on the table, smiling his mirthless grin, sat Lester.

Gram's cheeks were sunken. The smile, skeletal. Her skin was lifeless and gray in the combined beams of our flashlights. The eyes that squinted back were not my grandmother's. Gram had bright, sky-blue eyes. They took in everything with a mixture of love, wisdom and light, and then sent it back. I knew those eyes intimately. For years, they had provided one of the few ways that she could communicate with me when she had no voice.

These eyes held no love, no understanding; these sunken, lifeless slits calculated and plotted and mocked and hated. He hated me for taking his family away, freeing them from his corrupt influence, his cruelty, from Hell. Now, though, my loved ones were paying the price of the one brave thing I'd ever done.

"Hey, little Kipper."

He sat there casually in her velour track suit. I wondered how much of my grandmother was still inside that body, and how we were going to beat him without killing her—or getting ourselves killed.

On the table in front of him stood four urns, black like the one in Sylvia's shop. He was still up to his old tricks.

"Get out of her," I whispered. I didn't yell. I didn't threaten. It was not a request.

He smiled again, patiently, as if I didn't understand. "Oh, I plan to. This one's pretty much used up, anyway. But you tell me. Where should I go? Your friend Max? She's strong, likes girls. I could last a good long time in there. How 'bout your girlfriend? She's sweet. The fun we could have together. Would you like that?" He winked at Jessie.

"What about me? I'm the one you want. I'm standing right here. Take me. Show me just how strong you are." I wanted a piece of him, so bad, I could smell it.

His smile disappeared.

"You can't, can you? You're tied to that stupid clover, the one thing you had to have, and now you belong to it. You say my grandma is used up. Okay. Then maybe we should just take that necklace off of her and throw it into the sea."

He stood up. Not slow and plodding, like Gram had been moving recently. He sprung up as though the chair had burned his ass.

"You're limited now. You're stuck to that bit of gold like a fly in sap, and it's gonna keep you from spreading your filth any further."

"You won't hurt your Gram, dear." He mocked her voice.

"He won't, but I will." Jessie stepped forward with the gun poised, her finger on the trigger.

"The mouse decides to squeak." His eyes widened, just a little.

"Jessie, what're you doing?" asked Max.

"I'm ending this. You gave me this gun because you couldn't do what was necessary. I can't take his shit anymore."

"Damn, Kip, you know how to pick 'em."

"Max?" I pleaded.

She stepped forward, raised the staff, and in the most commanding voice she could muster, said, "Lester, begone. Retreat to the golden charm and trouble us no more."

Lester looked confused. Amused. He smiled.

"It was worth a try." She tossed the staff to me and strode forward, hefting her steel flashlight. "Time for you to go back into the pit, asshole."

He snarled and launched at her, moving too fast to follow with my light, bowling into her before she could even get to the table, then rammed her into the wall. Max's breath exploded out of her.

He grabbed her head and slammed it into the plaster, again and again.

I seemed to split in two. One part of me stood rooted to the ground, frozen. The other watched the entire scene play out from above. *Do something*, it whispered.

I rushed forward, tackling Lester and sending us both tumbling across the room. We landed in a heap on the filthy cold floor. I jammed the staff under his chin, pinning him to the ground. He grabbed me by the throat with both hands. Lightning quick they crawled around to the back of my neck.

There was a charge, as if a circuit had closed. Rage filled me. The world took on a crystal clarity. Gram lay helpless beneath me, barely conscious. I pulled the scepter back to drive it into her head.

An explosion sounded behind me as pain tore through my arm. I leapt to my feet and spun. Jessie, that sweet little thing, faced me with the gun quivering in her hands, tears streaming down her face. I surged toward her.

She fired again. Sparks erupted as the bullet struck the ground on my left. Then I was on her. I swung the club hard, sending the gun across the room..

"Sam?" She held her damaged hands out in front of her.

That's it, bitch. Beg. I brought the club around again. The wood tingled as it smacked the side of her head, crumpling her to the floor. I stepped forward and swung downward. The wood connected solidly again with a muted thud.

Yes! I was finally ending this bullshit.

My head snapped back, and at the same time, something grabbed my throat. It jerked again and again, biting into my neck.

It snapped.

The world lost its sharpness. My rage evaporated. I stood in that dark room, confused.

"What happened?"

The fight had spun me around and I stood now, looking at Max, her eyes wide. I couldn't read her expression. Shock, maybe? Blood trickled from a gash in the side of her forehead. In her gloved hand, she clutched the necklace.

I followed her gaze to the floor where Jessie lay. Blood seeped from the side of her head, soaking her light brown hair as it streamed to the floor. Forgotten, the scepter echoed hollowly as it dropped from my fingertips and fell to the floor.

14

THE HOSPITAL

THE FLUORESCENT LIGHTS IN THE WAITING ROOM CAST A harsh glare, making everything look ill.

The automatic doors opened, and the doctor approached through them. He looked exhausted, defeated. We got up to meet him.

"Your grandmother's in the ICU. She's very weak."

I couldn't find my voice. Max jumped in. "What about Jessie?"

He shook his head. "I'm sorry. Are you family?"

I couldn't respond. Stuck in my own head, I turned and stepped away.

He continued talking to Max. "If you could provide her contact information, we'll contact her family."

"Why don't you all get some sleep. It looks like you could use it." He started to leave, then paused.

"In cases of assault, we have to notify the police. They've dispatched an officer to come by and ask you some questions." With that, he left.

"That's all we fucking need," Max said under her

breath. She came over and hugged me, which was a rare thing for her. "How're you doing?"

"I need to take a piss." My mind was numb. Jessie was dead. Gram might die. I couldn't be here.

"Okay."

I had no idea where the men's room was. I didn't care. I beelined for the exit, not bothering to see if Max saw or not. I stepped out into a colder, darker night, making for Max's truck, and tore open the door.

Her pack was on the floor of the cab. I dumped it out on the seat. There was the gun, her wallet, other things - so much crap. The necklace wasn't there.

I unzipped the front compartment and pulled out whatever I found: lipstick, screwdriver, eyeshadow, folding knife. My hand closed around an incredibly thin chain and pulled it out.

The hospital doors opened behind me.

"Sam, no!"

Gripped tight in my fist, the clover shined dully in the night.

Again, power shot through me, and again, my world changed.

The Rain poured down hard on my head as I stood upon Lighthouse Rock. The drops pounded down from the sky like soggy pebbles as the wind howled past me. A massive wave smashed into the rock, shaking the ground and throwing spray high into the air.

I fought my way to the door. As before, the knob wouldn't turn. I used both hands and pushed as hard as I could, but it wouldn't release. I threw my shoulder into it, kicked it. It wouldn't budge. Nothing was going to stop me. I found a rock roughly the size of my fist and hammered the knob with it. Then I dropped it, and with both hands, turned it with all my strength. The corroded metal ripped at my skin, but finally, it budged. I leaned into the door and pushed. Cold and soaking wet, I stepped back into the main room.

It was dark like always. The smell was the same, too. I knew it wasn't real, and yet it was. Everything looked, smelt, sounded and felt exactly as it had before.

The plaster rocks crackled under my wet shoes as I strode across the room toward the rotunda.

"Lester, Where the fuck are you?" I yelled.

I crossed the room, and stepped into the rotunda below the lantern room. My foot crossed the threshold and met nothing. No floor, just space. Where there had been solid ground before, there was now a massive hole, and into it I fell.

The darkness through which I hurtled was absolute. Wind whipped past my face. It was the only clue that I was falling. My body tensed, anticipating the inevitable impact, but it didn't come.

I continued to plunge deeper into the pit, unable to keep track of time or distance.

Memories raced through my mind. I thought about my first climb up Lighthouse Rock, and how scared I'd been. I thought about Gram, lying helpless in a hospital bed, and Jessie, lying dead at my feet.

I thought about how my fear had led me to this. I knew I was going to die. I hoped Jessie would be waiting there, at the end.

And still I fell.

I spread my arms to slow my decent. I'd heard once that a skydiver had saved his own life that way, after his parachute had failed to open. The rushing wind pushed back, as it whistled through my hands.

I thought about how little time I'd had with Jessie, and how much better my life would've been if I hadn't let my fear keep me from making friends, taking chances, standing up for myself. What might we have been if we'd had more time? We'd been cheated of so much.

I thought about how much I loved my gram and my grandpa, and wondered if he'd be there at the end.

I thought about my parents, and how angry I was that they'd died so long ago. I remembered the night of the accident, and how, as our car hurtled down off the road, my mother had reached back over the seat for me, as I watched the ocean grow larger in the windshield.

I thought about Max and how lonely my life would've been if we hadn't met.

I had time to think about these things and more, as I plummeted farther and farther from home and everything I knew.

After a time, I wondered if I was really falling at all. Was it just a wind whipping by me in the dark? Was it a dream, or some hallucination Lester'd invented to scare me? He knew my fears, after all. I wondered if maybe I'd already died and this was the passage to the next life, and then I questioned whether I'd lived at all, or if that had been merely a dream.

I smacked hard, hitting the ground with such an impact that I bounced, sending a shockwave through my body and knocking the breath from my lungs, then I landed again and stayed there.

I lay prostrate on the ground, fighting to breathe, wheezing, forcing my lungs to open. Breath fled my body as quickly as I'd sucked it in. This felt familiar.

I opened my eyes as I struggled. A dim light greeted my gaze. My ragged lungs still strived to inhale.

Slowly, I drew a leg up underneath me. It hurt, but seemed to work. I brought up the other and rested for a time on my knees. After a while, I got my hands beneath me and pushed myself up. They sunk into the spongy, rust-colored powder that made up the ground. I turned my head one way and then the other. Everything seemed to work. Carefully, I stood, willing my lungs to inhale and exhale, over and over again.

I was in a massive cavern. The walls arched over, high above me, glowing with a soft light that revealed a world I could never have imagined.

Directly above was the opening through which I'd fallen, impossible to reach, even if I'd had the tallest ladder ever built.

Stalactites jabbed down from the ceiling, huge teeth drooling some kind of liquid, striking the soft ground around me with an irregular rhythm.

A long distance away lay the cavern's end. Moving slowly at first, I made for it.

I didn't know if this was real, or some sort of riddle, or a metaphor for my life. Had Lester created it? His attacks were always direct, savage. If this was his doing, it was more ambitious than anything he had tried before. No, this was something else. For all I knew, I was walking through Hell.

Apart from the water dripping down from the ceiling, I was the only thing that moved. Scattered everywhere were the bleached shells and brittle bones of thousands of sea creatures, half-sunken into the soft ground.

The end seemed miles away. Despite the size of the place, I felt an oppressive weight upon me, claustrophobic, as the air grew warm and moist. Drops splashed occasionally on my head and trickled down the back of my shirt.

My thoughts were of Jessie and Gram, and Max's dad, and little Suzie, and so forth, people Lester had hurt or killed. I didn't care what he threw at me. I was going to end this. Whatever this was, illusion or not, it would not keep me from making him pay. I'd never been so single-minded before.

Trudging through the cavern, replaying all our encounters, I thought of the last vision, of how he'd been forced to kill his own father - at least that's what he believed. I didn't doubt that his father had abused him, but everything he'd ever shown had been from his own point of view.

Did he really feel that by attacking others, bending them to his will, torturing them, he was getting revenge for the things that'd been done to him?

Whatever - I didn't care. It didn't matter. Plenty of people had tough lives. Maybe everybody did.

My hands bunched into fists as I walked - clenching and unclenching. I was going to tear that smug smile off his pale, pitted face.

Time passed, but it was impossible to guess how much. I didn't get hungry or thirsty or tired. I kept trudging forward, not knowing if I was heading in the right direction. Not knowing if there *was* a right direction.

Sea creatures weren't the only corpses half-buried in the ground. I passed the occasional human skeleton as well, their bones bent, broken, or separated by time to form grotesque caricatures, almost laughable in the way they were arranged now.

I looked up from the ground. I'd made good time while I'd been musing, if in fact, time moved at all here. I could now make out three openings in the wall.

I picked up my pace. As I walked, I imagined what life would've been like had my parents lived: the birthdays, Christmases, vacations, things we could've done. It made me happy and sad at the same time. My grandfather, who'd died just a couple of years ago, had taught me so much in that tiny fishing boat - just the two of us, floating in the bay, talking about life. "Always drive into the waves," he'd said. "Face them head on." He would share his memories, his knowledge. "Red sky at morning, sailors take warning."

And finally, I thought about Jessie - my first girlfriend. The only girl who'd ever seemed genuinely interested in me. What would our lives have been like if she'd lived? Would we have stayed together? Gotten married? Had kids?

The openings stood before me now. Three massive tunnels leading into the dark. They were each the same, with no differences I could make out, so I took the one on the right. No hesitation, no second thoughts, no deep breath.

I simply walked to the threshold and stepped through.

15

A LONG TIME COMING

WHAT LITTLE LIGHT THERE'D BEEN, VANISHED. THERE WAS no sense of falling. No feeling of hot or cold. No sound. No sensations at all.

It was as if, by stepping into the cave, I'd walked away from everything.

I felt lost.

I was conscious of being myself, but without physical form, I was reduced to an emotion, and that feeling was, as usual, fear.

If purgatory was real, this is what it would be - a state of not being - total and complete isolation.

It felt like I screamed in constant silence for years, or I think I did, for there was no vibration in my body, desperate for a glimmer or whisper or even an itch - something outside of me to show that I existed. Everything was nothing, and I couldn't shut it out. I may have lost my mind. Finally, after what seemed an eternity, I sensed a slight, subtle lessening of the dark. Everything shifted from black to less black, and then to not-quite gray.

My screams ceased as more levels of reality were

added: shapes, and then shadows and textures, and finally depth and solidity. It was cold.

I stood in a room. It became fully formed, with no colors. Just gradations of gray. The space seemed old, run down. Dirt and cobwebs marred the walls, with holes punched in them for good measure.

I shared this space with another - a boy sitting by himself on a wooden stool, looking out his lonely window. His shoulders slumped. He looked defeated.

I followed his line of sight. Outside, all was turmoil - a swirling, raging, colorless storm of incomprehensible shapes, writhing in a chaotic battle. If my previous reality was the manifestation of fear, then this was anger. Raw, brutal, world-devouring rage.

I approached the boy and knelt. His face was slack, bereft of emotion. A generic mask. Two eyes, a nose, below that, a mouth. Nothing distinctive or unique. Lester.

Just moments ago, I had wanted to kill this person. To end him painfully and permanently. Now, I couldn't help but pity him.

I rested a hand on his shoulder.

The window blew open, and the storm sucked me outside, buffeted by a chaotic maelstrom. Then this too took on a shape, coalescing into a figure standing opposite me: tall, slovenly, a stained shirt stretched tight across the belly. Lester's father. He came at me with a belt, lashing my body and head. I tried to shield myself, but there was nothing I could do. Blows hit me from different directions all at once. The buckle seared my skin, ripping strips from my body. I couldn't escape the pain - all-encompassing, beating and ripping and tearing.

It all stopped abruptly, and I lay huddled - drawn within myself. My arms shielded my head. After a time, I worked up the courage to peer out. The blackness had returned. Then another radical, sudden change, and I stood now in an old-fashioned kitchen. Like the room before, it lacked color - as if I were inside an old movie.

Three figures appeared before me: Susie, her sister Elisabeth, and their mom - Lester's wife. Silently, they turned their backs and, holding hands, walked away. Abandoning me.

Everything changed again, and now the kitchen was replaced by the lighthouse. This time, it was the members of the crew that Lester had killed. James Calloway; the Head Lighthouse Keeper, as well as Abrams and Torkson, standing over me with looks of derision on their faces. They pointed down at me and laughed, throwing in vicious kicks for good measure. I felt their superiority as they ridiculed me from the heights. Their abuse hit me like his father's belt. It caused physical pain from which I couldn't escape. It broke off, and again, I found myself in a state of nothing.

The lighthouse appeared around me again, and I could have been looking at a mirror, for the figure I saw now was me. I watched myself stroll through the colorless rooms like a tourist. Then I encountered Susie, Lester's daughter, all bright and shining and young. Her curly blond hair framed her innocent face. My double knelt and spread his arms wide. Susie ran joyfully into his embrace. He picked her up and spun her around.

Instead of joy, I felt abandoned, betrayed.

I knew now where I was. Somehow, I had crossed a line into Lester himself. Rather than viewing the scenes he selected, I viewed life symbolically the way he saw it.

Tortured by his father. Abused by his crew. Abandoned by his family.

In his world, he was a victim. And I saw now that the power he took from others was the only real interaction he'd ever experienced. To him, it was almost intimate. He longed to feel the touch of another.

When he killed, he felt it was justified. An act of self-defense.

In this twisted, joyless world, his attacks were rebellious acts of heroism.

All this time, his belief fueled his rage at a world that was out to get him, or worse, discard him. The crop that his father had sown so long ago had born fruit. His strength was, in fact, his greatest weakness. It was his fear of being alone, of being a victim, abandoned.

Now, I knew how to beat him.

In this world, I was just a thought, but with free will. I had to use it while I had it.

I closed my eyes and summoned the first vision I'd experienced.

Two little girls played in the front yard, chasing each other with a garden hose. The water glittered in the sun. Their mom came out and joined them. They giggled and screamed joyfully under a brilliant blue sky.

Lester appeared, and the colors drained away.

He looked the way he saw himself: small, scrawny, ugly. His face, a mask of pits and scars. His thin red hair clung tight to his skull.

I took control. With focus, Lester took Suzie's place; a sweet, six-year-old who knew nothing of her father but fear. I morphed into him, but not the way he pictured himself - not the weak victim. No, I was huge, powerful, looming over the three girls with my weathered clothes and rotten teeth. My face was not that of an abused boy, instead it wore the ruddy complexion of a ruthless, threatening tyrant. I followed them inside and replayed the scene as I remembered, highlighting the terror he had imposed.

He watched as I attacked the image of his wife; delivering a savage blow to the stomach that dropped her to the ground. I beat her exactly as he'd done.

I willed Annie, the youngest daughter, to come at me in a brave, foolish, childish attempt to save her mother. Her tiny fists beat impotently on my legs. And, just as he had done, I threw her against the wall. With a sickening thud, she crumpled to the floor.

"No," he cried, "That's not how it happened."

I regarded him with his own savage face and replied in his voice, "You sure about that, little Kipper?"

His wife scooped up their daughter, limp in her arms, and sprinted for the door. I grabbed her arm and jerked her back inside.

Lester bolted outside. His bare little girl's feet flew over the grass, then slapped the pavement beyond. I rushed out after and caught him. With a heart-sickening wrench, I snapped his little neck.

The scene went black. He again appeared before me in the form that he saw himself. A young boy; abused, neglected, weak.

"You believed you were powerless. You refused to see who you really were. You could have made a different choice."

"All I did—" he said.

"All you did was soak in your own self-pity and hurt people. That's your legacy."

"How can you stop me?" He smiled.

"I don't have to. You've seen the truth."

"Like hell." He charged. A small, rusty blade suddenly appeared in his hand. I let him come. The blade pierced my skin, ripped my organs, freed my blood. He stabbed and hacked and slashed again and again and again.

I fell to the ground in an expanding red pool. Parting my dying lips, I whispered, "See what you've become?"

My eyes closed. The world receded. I could finally stop fighting.

A presence appeared next to me, warm and soft and loving. She took my face in her hands and kissed me.

"Jessie?"

"I'm here."

"Are we done? Am I going to be with you?"

She smiled. "Not quite yet." She took my hand, and my wounds healed. She pulled me to my feet.

We found ourselves back in the darkened lighthouse. Lester morphed into Jessie, standing terrified, with the gun in her hands. Jessie, cloaked as a possessed version of me, charged, swung the scepter, and smacked the gun away. As Lester stood, shaking and crying in his fear, she struck again, sending him to the floor. She swung the club down, and with a last crack, ended it.

It may have been play-acting, a sort of supernatural puppet show, but the pain was real and the lesson was clear. "Now, you know what you are," she said.

As Gram used to say, all bullies get their come-uppance.

The scepter disappeared, as did Lester Tod and the lighthouse.

We stood together - Jessie and I - on the beach, as we'd done that one perfect evening not so long ago, and, holding hands, we kissed in the miraculous light of the setting sun.

"Is it done? For real?" I asked, not daring to believe.

She looked up into my eyes. "He's beaten. He'll linger for a time, but eventually, he'll crossover." She squeezed my fingers. "In the meantime..." she kissed me again, soft and warm, and then sighed as she rested her head against my chest. "You have to go back. They need you."

I wanted to argue, but I couldn't speak. A tear dripped down my cheek.

"We'll be together. I promise." She took me into her arms and we embraced as if it was the last time.

I opened my eyes. Max stood over me, blocking the night sky. Dim light glinted off the piercings in her face and ears, as tears streamed down her cheeks. A snot bubble dangled from her nose. "Sam? Sam! It fucking better be you!"

"Yeah, Max, it's me."

"What were you thinking?"

"He's done."

"Lester?"

I nodded.

All sobs and tears and mucus. She gathered me up and held me tight. "It's over?"

"Yeah, it's over."

EPILOGUE - A NEW BEGINNING

THE FOUR OF US, MAX, GRAM, BUNNY (MAX'S STEP-mother), and I, huddled together on the deck of The Sea Witch, a fishing boat we'd chartered for the morning. Although the sun streamed down on the sparkling water, we wore coats to keep out the chill ocean wind.

We idled for a moment, then the motor went silent.

I asked, "Is this the place?"

The captain called back, "The trench is right below us. You can come look at the sonar if you want."

"I trust you," I said.

"Fucked if I do. Show me," Max murmured, and headed to the cabin to double check our position.

We were parked outside the bay, floating over the deepest part of Monterey Canyon, a massive submarine chasm that plunged miles beneath the surface.

Gram sat on a bench, her hand resting on a cane. She inhaled the crisp air. "I'd forgotten how beautiful it could be out here. You know, your grandpa used to take me out fishing back when we were younger."

"Maybe we can go out together sometime," I said.

She smiled. "That would be nice."

Max hollered from the cockpit. "He's right. We're here." She hurried back to join us.

"Should we say a few words?" Bunny asked.

"How about 'good fucking riddance.'" said Gram.

We shared a quiet chuckle.

A large presence loomed over me, blocking out the sun, as a massive, calloused hand grabbed my own. "Maybe we should just pray for peace," said the first mate in a rough voice, as he took his place next to me.

Max took this in and shot me a surprised look. "What the hell —?"

I smiled. "She didn't want to miss it."

"Jessie?"

Smiling, the fisherman nodded.

Her eyes filling with tears, Max engulfed the huge man in her arms.

Surprised, Jessie stumbled back, then smiled and returned the hug.

I watched the reunion for a moment, reveling in the fact that sometimes, goodbyes weren't as final as they seemed. Then I took a deep breath and said, "It's time."

A hush fell over us as I reached into a plain paper shopping bag I'd stowed under my arm and drew out the urn. I unscrewed the top and poured out the contents. For just a moment, the clover dangled from my fingers, glimmering gold in the clear sunlight - a final taste of life - then I dropped it back inside, replaced the lid nice and tight, and giving a silent prayer, let it fall.

It entered the water with a gentle splash, leaving as evidence only delicate ripples dancing toward the horizon as it fell away, disappearing down, into the depths.

A NOTE FROM THE AUTHOR

Thank you so much for reading **Into the Depths**.

If you have the time, and the inclination, it would mean the world if you leave a review on Amazon, letting me, and the world know how you felt about it.

Independent writers depend on our readers to spread the word about our work. I mean, who's gonna listen to me? I wrote the thing.

Anyway, thank you again, for reading. If you enjoyed it, you can find my other titles on Amazon.

ABOUT THE AUTHOR

D.L. Strand has been - among other things - an entrepreneur, a coffee roaster, and a filmmaker. He's worked on various film and TV productions around the United States, including the movie *Us* with Jordan Peele and the TV comedy *Abbott Elementary* with Quinta Brunson, but is happiest when he's at home, sitting in his jammy pants in front of his computer, dreaming up truly awful things.

Storyteller's Pub
For news and updates - join the Storyteller's Pub Newsletter at:
storytellerspub.com

Like Audiobooks?
Find free audio versions of D.L.'s stories (read by the author) on his podcast, **Storyteller's Pub**, at:
https://podcasters.spotify.com/pod/show/dlstrand

OTHER TITLES BY D.L. STRAND

Novellas:
Into the Storm - Tales From the Lightouse, Book 1
Into the Dark - Tales From the Lighthouse, Book 2

Short Fiction:
Catch - A Storyteller's Pub Horrifying Short
Fetch - A Storyteller's Pub Horrifying Short
The Garden - A Storyteller's Pub Horrifying Short

www.ingramcontent.com/pod-product-compliance
Lightning Source LLC
Chambersburg PA
CBHW052015170626
46808CB00007B/2938